The ring

I am sorry for all girls, Emily thought, because all of us love boys.

She felt the ring on the fourth finger of her left hand. In that tiny gold circle were all the plans so carefully, lovingly made since New Year's Eve when Matt had placed it there.

All gone. All meaningless.

For Matt had had a better offer.

SUMMER NIGHTS

CAROLINE B. COONEY

SCHOLASTIC INC.
New York Toronto London Auckland Sydney

Cover Photo by David Turner

ISBN 0-590-45786-1

Copyright © 1988 by Caroline B. Cooney.
All rights reserved. Published by Scholastic Inc.
POINT is a registered trademark of Scholastic Inc.

12 11 10 9 8 7 6 5 4 3 2 1   6   2 3 4 5 6 7/9

Printed in the U.S.A.   01

Prologue

The girls were slick with sun-block lotion and the air smelled of coconut oil. The radio played softly, the wind blew gently, and the heat of August soaked into their hearts and minds. There was a party to get ready for, but since the guest of honor didn't know about it, conversation was difficult.

For high school was over, graduation a memory, and Anne would be the first to leave Westerly the following morning. How unlike Anne to be first! It gave the girls a shiver, because already they could see that the neat little predictions written under their yearbook photographs might not turn out as planned.

They lay in the sun thinking of the surprise party on the boat: the shining river and the fireworks after dark. They thought of the dresses they would wear and the boys who would be there.

Boys.

Always — whether you thought of today or tomorrow, college or commuting, you thought also of boys.

Chapter 1

The timer went off with a gentle ding. The girls rolled over so they would tan evenly. The sun's strength was fading now, though, and the shadows from the trees by the back steps had reached Beth's feet. The banana and yogurt Beth Rose had had for lunch felt very long ago. She wondered what they would have to eat at the party. Steak, broiled on charcoal at the beach? Or hot dogs and hamburgers? Or was it being catered, so they risked eggplant parmesan? She was in an eating mood. There was nothing like a yogurt and banana to put a girl in an eating mood.

Beth Rose had dark red hair and transparent skin with an ever-increasing array of light freckles. She was not at her best in the sun. She lay on her stomach now, resting her face on her crossed hands, and admired the tans of the other girls. Anne, of course, was perfect, having tanned an even gold. Anne's normally blonde hair had become nearly silver over the summer, until she was almost a walking beach scene. Golden sun and white-hot sand were the colors of Anne's body. Even half asleep on the hot gray slates that formed a wide terrace around the swimming pool, Anne seemed warmer and more intense than the rest of them. She was not leaving till the next day, but already she had a star's quality.

I want to be a star, too, thought Beth Rose. But I don't know that I want to take on the whole world. One single terrific boy would do. Maybe tonight on the boat, I'll meet a boy who is perfect for me.

Beth Rose sighed. She had often met boys who were perfect for her. They, regrettably, had not considered Beth Rose perfect for them. Besides, there would be no strangers on the boat tonight, only people she had known forever.

Beth could hardly wait for the signal from Kip to get moving on the surprise party plans. She could not imagine how the rest of them endured it — lying around getting tan when there was a party ahead. She wanted to talk of boys and dresses and dancing and life. They just snoozed away as if it were any old summer afternoon.

It was very hot.

The heat seemed to slow time down, the hours growing heavier and longer.

Beth Rose closed her eyes and dreamed of boys. She felt like a war strategist rather than a dreamer, but that was how it was with boys. You had to plan your moves. The other girls were leaving the battlefield. Anne circling the globe, Kip going to college in New York, Emily getting married.

Beth Rose did not know how all this had come about. It was as if she had gone to get an ice-cream cone or to have her hair cut, and in the same half hour everybody else made plans for life and bought plane tickets.

Everybody was so impressed with Anne's job, so full of excitement about what Anne would be doing. I am a hick, thought Beth. I don't envy Anne. I have no desire to see Paris or Rome. I want a boyfriend and some new clothes.

She toyed with the idea of Con being her boyfriend, since Anne was dumping him in preference of London and Tokyo. But why should Con forget perfect, golden Anne — like a shining dove in flight — to take out plain, old, red-haired Beth Rose? Plus, of course, being one of Anne's confidants, Beth knew that Con might be the most handsome, suave and dashing boy in the high school, but he was not the nicest. In fact, for a guy with a ten body, it was too bad he was about a three on a nice scale.

"This," said Molly from her side of the pool, "is the kind of afternoon when it feels as if something special is about to happen." Molly was wearing a tiny bathing suit which she had rolled down to make even tinier, and

5

when she propped herself up on her elbow it was to admire her own figure. Molly did a slow scissors kick and left one leg up to admire it framed against the blue sky.

Something special *was* going to happen, of course, but not to Molly. Nobody would invite Molly anywhere, let alone to Anne's surprise party. Molly was petty, mean, and borderline-criminal, and why Anne even let Molly into her yard was a mystery to Beth. Probably so full of daydreams she forgot who Molly is, thought Beth. I think Anne has even forgotten who Con is. Con won't like that at all.

"We could crash the dance they're giving over in Raulston," Molly suggested.

So that was why she had come. To find company for party crashing. How odd that she picked us, Beth thought. She knows we can't stand her and I would have said it was mutual.

"Too hot to party," Kip mumbled.

Molly snorted. She knew perfectly well it was never too hot to party.

"A hundred and eight degrees out," Beth agreed, with mild exaggeration. "We don't want to die of heat prostration the day before we turn into adults." This silenced Molly. But Beth did not feel as if she were turning into an adult. The only thing Beth was turning into was a slightly more sunburned teenager than she had been yesterday. Beth was positively exhausted by the energy her friends had. Her own plans included nothing new. She would take biology and English at the junior college while she waitressed at Pizza Hut.

It was a mistake, she thought. Commuting is not a threshold. Nothing changes. Nobody will give *me* a good-bye party. I'm not going anywhere.

What if that's true all my life?

What if I never go anywhere?

Maybe I'm already as sophisticated and knowledgeable as I'm ever going to be.

If that's true, Beth thought, I might as well roll over into the swimming pool and breathe chlorinated blue water.

Only two years before Beth Rose had been an ugly duckling, blossoming overnight at the Autumn Leaves Dance with Gary. Maybe I'm going back into the ugly duckling's shell, she thought. It was magic, but the spell is broken. The old pieces of shell are still lying there, waiting to snap shut on me.

Suddenly the thought of staying in Westerly was oppressive, even frightening. Life was a dark alley.

Beth Rose sat up quickly and moved back into the sunlight.

"What's the matter?" Molly asked, amused. "Ghost walk on your grave?"

Molly could always laugh at people in pain. Beth stared at Molly, trying to detect Molly's plan, her reason for coming there. But the sun was in Beth's eyes and Molly just looked like another teenager in a skimpy bikini, worrying about her tan.

Molly is jealous of us, Beth Rose thought. She's jealous of Kip, going to a terrific school; and Emily, whose boyfriend wants them to get married; and Anne, who is going to see the world. If Molly knew about the surprise party, she'd want it to be for her. She'd *make* it be for her. But nobody cares enough about Molly to say good-bye. Not one of us here has even asked Molly what she's going to do this fall.

How jealous is she? Beth Rose wondered. Jealous enough to — to do something?

Chapter 2

Anne Stephens tanned an even gold. The thin straps of her bikini top were tucked in so that her shoulders would get no white stripes. The pale pastel of her swimsuit looked like ice against her skin. She lay directly on the dark gray slate that made a path around the swimming pool in her backyard. She loved the deep heat of the stones, soaking into her bones and giving her strength. She was going to need a lot of that to get through the rest of the day.

There was a certain joy in being beautiful. Anne liked being admired. She liked looking in a mirror. But there was a certain agony in it, also. People did not look beyond the beauty. Anne could be upset, but people would tell her how nice her hair looked. Anne could be screaming inside, but people would say how becoming that color was on her. Anne could be sick with fear, but people would say, You know, you should be a model.

9

Right now Anne was filled with rage and not one of the other four girls suspected a thing. Nobody saw her moods. It was as if beauty was supposed to put you beyond bad moods. A glamorous girl had no right to feel rotten and, if she did, she should keep quiet about it.

It was her parents she was mad at.

How could they raise a daughter, teach her right and wrong, teach her to say Thank you and Please, to brush her teeth, study hard, and cross the street only at corners . . . and then spend her last weeks at home telling her she was no good?

Anne, dear, you were just hired because of your looks. You have no background for this. You've never organized anything in your life. Your friend Kip could do this job well. But you? Darling, it's not too late to back out. Why don't you telephone Miss Glynn right now and say you've decided against it?

Anne, dear, your head is going to be turned by all those glossy, glitzy people. You won't be able to withstand the pressures.

Anne, you'll have to manage so much money. Your judgment isn't very good, you know. What if you find yourselves in Japan or Australia and you have no money because you've spent it all on silly souvenirs?

Anne, dear, a whole year? Why, you were so homesick at camp we had to go get you on the fourth night.

And when Anne, dear, did not give in to

criticism, they began offering her bribes. *If you stay home, dear, Daddy will buy you your first car.*

And when Anne, dear, resisted even the bribes, they began to tell her it wouldn't be any fun, anyhow. Anne, dear, you realize you won't actually see anything of those great romantic cities? You'll just be in airports, hotel lobbies, and *more* airports and hotel lobbies.

Under the hot August sun Anne's skin turned more golden.

But her thoughts burned and burned.

Emily struggled to keep total control. It was imperative not to break down. This was Anne's last day and Emily must not turn the attention on herself. That would be selfish.

Emily yearned to be selfish. She wanted to leap to her feet, screaming and sobbing and gathering them round her to comfort her and agree that Matthew O'Connor should be killed in a long drawn-out painful manner.

But Anne was her best friend. Emily believed firmly she had a duty to her best friend to keep the whole night on a cheerful happy level.

She made herself think about the party. The *Duet* was a lovely tubby boat that took tourists from Westerly to Swallow Island and back. Burnished brass rails surrounded a deck large enough to dance on, and loden-green paint gleamed on a cabin large enough to lounge in. She wondered how much the party would cost Con and why his parents allowed it. Nobody else had mentioned the practicalities of such a lavish send-off. Could it really be true that Con had arranged fireworks? Why, whole towns had to struggle to raise money for fireworks!

Emily fidgeted with her towel, and Beth Rose smiled at her as if to start a conversation. Any conversation with Beth Rose would be about boys. Emily could not talk about boys right now. Certainly not about her *own* boy. Emily blinked hard to keep the tears from rolling down her cheeks.

"Why, Em," Beth said, "is something wrong?"

"No, no. Allergy. Humid air. Affects me like this." Emily lay down and put the towel solidly over her eyes to soak up the tears. Her tears hurt, as if they were acid poured in there by some villain.

"Do you think Gary will be there?" Beth Rose whispered to her, so Anne could not hear.

Em felt sorry for Beth, still fond of Gary. They had studied a poem in English Lit. "No man is an island." Well, John Donne was wrong. Gary *was* an island, complete with rivers on all sides and no bridges. Nobody would ever possess Gary and Gary would never try to possess anyone, either. He was content to be alone or on the fringes.

But then, thought Emily Edmundson, I

am sorry for all girls, because all of us love boys.

She felt the ring on the fourth finger of her left hand. In that tiny gold circle were all the plans so carefully, lovingly made since New Year's Eve when Matt had placed it there.

All gone. All meaningless.

For Matt had had a better offer.

Chapter 3

Beth Rose could not stand it any longer. It was driving her crazy, this gathering. Anne stayed suspended in a dream; Emily and Kip either slept or pretended to; Molly forced her bright, sharp chatter on people who didn't like her.

"Oh, my gosh!" Beth jumped up, stumbling over her own towel. "I forgot the ice cream."

Kip glared at her. Emily slept on.

Anne said, "What ice cream?"

Molly's eyes narrowed.

Beth said, "My family. We're — having this big summer thing — uh — tomorrow — and I was supposed to drive over to Benjie's and get homemade ice cream. I've got to run." There. She'd handled it well. Nobody would suspect Beth Rose was responsible for bringing the ice cream to the good-bye party. Beth slipped into her white jeans and sleeveless T, slithered her toes into sandals and headed for her car parked out front.

Anne cried out, "Bethie! Beth, where are you going? I'm not going to see you later. I'm leaving in the morning."

"I forgot," Beth said guiltily. "I mean, I didn't forget, it's just that the whole idea of you going abroad for a year — I can't get a grip on it, Anne. I can't believe it's actually tomorrow."

Anne's silvery shiver of laughter matched her hair. She'll never come home, Beth Rose thought. She's going to be among stars and she's going to become a star. No wonder Con is throwing this huge party in a last-ditch attempt to keep her home. He knows that once the world has seen Anne, she'll belong to the world, not to him.

Anne hugged Beth fiercely. "Oh, Bethie, to think that two years ago you and I had never even spoken. We were so lucky we met at that dance. It feels like years ago. I feel like you and I have been friends forever and ever and ever."

It was a strange, unsuccessful good-bye. Beth knew they would say it all over again in a few hours, but Anne didn't. And for all that Anne was sorry and would miss Beth, Beth could feel Anne shaking with excitement, her mind already gone, waiting for her body and clothes to catch up.

I will never forget Anne, Beth thought. But she will forget me.

That made Beth cry, and tears from Beth seemed to satisfy Anne, so they were able to break loose. Beth got into her car and drove quickly off, stopping around the corner to search for a Kleenex and mop up her tears before she went on.

Kip Elliott was filled with the joy of going to college soon.

For all those long high school years, she had struggled for good grades, run committees, chaired activities, and played on teams. She had read hundreds of college catalogs and filled out dozens of forms. She had taken SAT exams and visited campuses and lived through interviews.

The long wait for acceptance was over. College began in ten days. She had her dorm assignment, her roommate had written, her trunk had been shipped — and New York, New York awaited the arrival of Kip Elliott!

She remembered how, on the day her acceptance arrived in the mail, she raced into school screaming, "I'm going to college in New York City!"

Nobody was thrilled. "Why do you want to do that?" they all said, frowning. "Don't you want to be on a real campus? Aren't you afraid of crime? Don't you worry about getting homesick?"

"No!" Kip shouted. "No, no, no, a thousand times no!" She'd spent her entire last month of high school trying to find a single graduating senior who thought she was lucky. But they were glad to be going to ordinary colleges close to home, with big maple trees and wide campus lawns, low brick dormitories, and other freshmen they knew from home.

How unfair it was to have worked so hard for something nobody else even wanted.

Kip was definitely ready to leave Westerly.

Kip leaped into the pool suddenly, splashing Emily. She did a swift stroke to one end and came more swiftly back, working off a little of the tremendous energy she always had.

Anne herself never went into the pool. The chlorine hurt her eyes too much. Kip lived in an apartment with four little brothers. It is symbolic of the unfairness of life, Kip thought, that the girl who hates swimming is the one who owns the pool.

Kip had always envied Anne. Anne was so pretty and popular, with Con always at her side arranging the next time they would be together. Anne had plenty of money and a truly enviable wardrobe. Of course, Con had a few drawbacks, number one being that he was a conceited jerk.

Yet Kip liked Con. She had to remind herself what a jerk he was or she forgot. He was charming and funny and always said the right compliment to make a girl feel good. Even Anne (who had more proof than anybody what a jerk Con was) fell time and time again under Con's charm.

Those two had started dating in seventh grade. You had only to look at this year's crop of seventh graders to know that it was a disgusting uncivilized age. Thirteen-year-old boys didn't seem capable of anything other than rude, crude, and socially unacceptable noises. Yet Con and Anne had begun even then setting an example of romance few had been able to match then or later. (Of course, there was the little lapse of Anne's pregnancy and then giving the baby up for adoption; few girls *wanted* to match that at age sixteen, and unmarried.)

It's good, Kip thought, that Anne is leaving. If she went on to State University with Con, Con would stay in charge and Anne would stay obedient. Anne will come back changed. She'll have spent a year doing things Con can't even imagine.

Even *I* can't imagine them, Kip thought, pushing her jealousy away, not letting herself think of foreign lands and fine hotels and fabulous star-studded gala parties.

I wish it were my good-bye party tonight, Kip thought, diving under one more time. I wish somebody had decided to give me a good-bye party.

She started crying underwater, a weird feeling, and when she surfaced her tears blended in with the pool water streaming out of her hair.

She forced her thoughts to college.

There would be, among other things, eighteen hundred boys in her class.

Now how, Kip asked herself, can I possibly live with a collection of one thousand eight hundred boys and not find at least a dozen absolutely perfect ones? Answer: I can't. So, in a matter of days, life is going to be boy-perfect.

Chapter 4

Anne walked slowly through her dark house
and back out to Kip, Emily, and Molly. When
you have been in the sun for hours, a house is
as dim as a cave, musty as an attic.

Not to see Beth for a year!

It did not seem possible to Anne, either.
None of them had ever been anywhere but
Westerly. To go more than a weekend without seeing all your friends was beyond com-
prehension.

The first doubt assailed Anne.

What am I doing? she thought.

She stared at the familiar backyard she
would not walk in for another twelve months.

I must stay calm. Less than twenty-four
hours now. I'll keep the girls here as long as
I can. Then I'll take a long time dressing for
my last date with Con. I'll stay with him till
midnight. When I come home I'll tell Mother
and Daddy I'm too tired to talk. As soon as

I'm up in the morning we have to leave for the airport. So they can't attack me much more.

And it's important not to fight at the very end. I won't want to leave to the sound of anger.

She wondered how much hugging and kissing there would be from Con. It was possible their date would be worse than staying home. Con was coming for her at seven. If this went like their last few dates, they would be back home at seven-ten.

Con actually thought Anne should have asked his permission before interviewing for this job. "I didn't even know!" Con had cried. "Other people had to tell me you were trying to get the job." He had stomped around, jamming his hands in and out of his jeans pockets. These days Con wore baggy pants, but when they started seeing each other in seventh grade, jeans were tight. Back then, Con couldn't have squeezed a lavatory pass into his pockets.

Anne, smiling at that memory, had said, "I'll never have a chance like this again, Con. You wouldn't want me to pass it up."

But he did. He thought the job would change her, turn her into a snob. It seemed the best strategy to joke about it. "You're right, Con," she said, laughing. "Probably I'll forget everybody. Have a whole new set of friends and travel only by Concorde and never land in Westerly." She tickled him lightly at the back of the neck where his hair grew down in a thick, dark wave.

Con had grabbed her arm roughly. "How can you throw away what's between us?" he demanded. "We're supposed to have the best romance in this whole high school. Weren't we voted Class Couple? We've lasted through thick and thin, Anne. You can't go now."

She had lasted through thick and thin. Con had chosen to spend the hard parts with Molly. Anne had forgiven him, but forgetting was harder. She sometimes wondered if she were the only person who remembered the little baby girl they had given away, the little girl who called other people Mommy and Daddy, the little girl who would be old enough, pretty soon, actually to say those words out loud.

Her parents could not bear the subject. Con pretended it had never happened. Her friends never referred to it. Anne thought of it every day.

She was not sure exactly what that had to do with her new job, but somehow it had been part of the final decision to take it.

Last May the local paper had carried an interview with a very elderly actress named Ivory Glynn, the only famous person ever born in the little city of Westerly. Fifty years before, a film called *Ivory Rose* had climaxed her fabulous career, and after *Ivory Rose*, Miss Glynn retired from Hollywood, while generation after generation of film goers remained her fans. Now, film festivals from Cannes to Buenos Aires to Los Angeles were going to feature the fiftieth anniversary of *Ivory Rose* and Miss Glynn, now age seventy-four, had emerged from seclusion and come to Westerly to find a companion to go with her around the world.

Con just laughed when he read the article. "Can you imagine traveling with that old biddy?" he scoffed. "Probably have to spend your time hunting down wheelchairs and flannel sheets and hot-water bottles."

That night Anne and Con were at Dory's, a large family-style restaurant on the river. It was one of the few places in Westerly where teenagers could hang out. You could buy one soda and dance half the night, or sit outside on benches, or just mill around, looking for people you knew.

"Now, listen to me, Anne," Con said that night. "I didn't like our dorm assignments at State, so I drove up there yesterday and had them changed. Took some talking, but I wrapped that woman in the student residence office around my finger and I got what I wanted."

Anne was not listening. London. Rome. Planes taking off, silver streaks in a blue sky. What a wonderful woman Ivory Glynn must be. Having stayed out of public sight all these years, brave enough to walk back on-stage.

"Now, what did you go and sign up for Music Literature for, Anne?" Con demanded. "You know what that is? Crap like Beethoven and Mozart and you have to sit in the music building all week listening to tapes. Drop that course, Anne, you won't like it. It'll take up too much of your time."

They leaned over the splintery railing and looked down into the Westerly River. Anne fed her potato chips to a flotilla of ducks. Those ducks have more purpose in life than I do, Anne thought. I'm not even paddling. I'm letting Con paddle for me.

Con informed her what tomorrow's plans would be.

Anne Stephens fed the ducks. She thought she would rather make her own plans for tomorrow. Perhaps she would rather make her own plans for all her tomorrows.

In the morning she arranged an interview with Ivory Glynn.

Miss Glynn was fragile, her skin very white, with deep wrinkles like crushed aluminum foil gently pulled back apart. Her hair was equally white and did not curl, but stuck up like escaped pillow stuffing. She was beautifully dressed, but she sat awkwardly against many pillows. A watch with a jeweled wristband dangled on a thin, blue-veined wrist.

"My dear," Ivory Glynn said to Anne, "you are quite amazingly lovely. You remind me of myself. But as you have never traveled,

I cannot begin to know how you might handle an emergency, and a girl of eighteen lacks the judgment I will need in a companion."

Anne flushed with embarrassment. How small-town it would be to mention her four years of high school French and three years of Spanish. Impossible to announce that after a lifetime of parental or boyfriend control, she was ready now to make decisions. Nor could she list those romantic cities like a travel brochure and say she hoped for a free ride from Miss Glynn.

The actress cleared her throat. Anne got up and poured her water from the carafe on the table. Miss Glynn offered Anne a Coke. "And perhaps you would tell me, as you sip it, why you would even *want* to go with me?" said Miss Glynn. "You are about to leave for college and the company of several thousand other teenagers away from home for the first time. Think of dorm life, campus life, freedom, and new friends!"

Anne smiled at her. "I know. I do think of it. I love to go into a roomful of strangers and know that soon they will have turned into friends."

Miss Glynn set her glass down. "Now that," she said, "is an extraordinary claim. Most people — I include myself — hate a roomful of strangers. Most people are afraid they will *never* break the barriers and have new friends."

"Oh, no." Anne shook her golden hair.

"I'm not the smartest at school. I don't have a flair for anything academic. But I can make friends. I could get off the plane with you, among all the world's strangers, and I would make friends. I might have to ask for help with taxis or menus, but I'd be all right because I'd make friends who'd help me." She blushed again. "I guess I can also waste people's time," she admitted. "I'm sorry I bothered you, Miss Glynn."

The old lady got to her feet. It did not appear to be an easy task. Anne helped her up and steadied her. "Old age," remarked Miss Glynn, "is lamentable."

They shook hands, Anne being careful not to apply pressure to the arthritic fingers.

And one week later, having interviewed people who wanted to meet other stars, people who wanted glamour to rub off on them, and people who hoped for money and fame themselves, Miss Glynn offered Anne the job, because Anne could make friends anywhere.

Anne sat back down by the pool, smiling at everybody. The hard part, she thought, is *keeping* friends!

I cannot have any arguments with anybody. It's not enough that I will be making friends overseas; I want to come back to friends here!

Chapter 5

Emily Edmundson thought of herself as a person with two definite stages, much as a tadpole will later be a frog. There was the pre-Matt Emily and then came the Matt-Emily.

Pre-Matt Emily was a nervous little girl with so little personality her teachers could never remember her name. Pre-Matt Emily had no close girlfriends even — just a cluster of other uninteresting girls with whom she generally had lunch.

But Matt met her out of town and had not been told she was boring. Matt was such an exciting, crazy, unthinking jock of a kid, he just swept her up into his personality, and they became a pair. Matt was always running, always talking, always full of plans and projects. He was a car freak. He'd been restoring and making money on old cars since he was barely fourteen. He had more energy than any other person Emily knew.

People loved to be around Matt. The moment Emily began dating him, she was grafted onto the social lives of people like Anne and Con, and Beth Rose and Gary, or Kip and whoever she was dating at the minute.

Her life in the last two years, her Matt-life, had been perfection.

Now, Matthew O'Connor had a peculiarity. In this one way he was different from any boy in the high school. A thousand other boys and not one of them ached to get married. To listen to them, you'd figure marriage as a social custom had vanished. Not for Matt. He actually looked forward to having a wife and family, his own house and his own business. He even said this out loud . . . to other boys.

On New Year's Eve, at the dance where so many exciting things happened to all the rest, the most exciting and terrifying thing imaginable happened to Emily. Matt gave her a diamond ring and asked her to marry him.

She was stunned, afraid. She hardly knew how to put the ring on. Or if she should.

We'll get married, Matt said, laughing in wild joy, we'll live happily ever after.

It took him months to convince her it was best, and then she fell into his daydream, and they planned together. Her doubts were gone; Matt was right, hadn't he always been right?

Then came the phone call.

"Em, Em, guess what! You'll never believe

what! But guess anyway. No, don't, because you won't. Just listen to me, are you listening to me?" Matt always talked like that. Emily laughed to hear him. No doubt the big excitement was because he got the new windshield into the Triumph on the first try.

"Jordan Saylor's racing team," Matt shouted. "You know Saylor, right? Saylor Oil? The biggest sponsor of car races in America? Saylor? You know it? Right?"

"I know it now," Emily agreed.

"Right, right. Emily, this car I restored, a guy on Saylor's pit team bought it. Pit team, Emily! Those are the guys that fix the racing cars right there on the track, changing tires in seconds, putting out fires, fixing gear shafts. *Saylor's*, Em!"

"That's pretty exciting," Emily said, who thought it was pretty boring.

"And they offered me a job."

She would always remember that, how the sentence lay there, sending off little facts like atoms bombing her helpless heart. There were no racetracks, no pit teams, no Saylor's within five hundred miles of Westerly. And race teams did not stay at one little track. They traveled with the cars. They were, quite literally, a road crew.

"A job?" Emily repeated.

It was a fabulous job, Matt told her. A perfect, unbelievable opportunity, one he could never pass up. So instead of opening his own garage to restore cars — well, he'd be going off as soon as possible to join the pit crew. They needed him today, actually, but he explained he couldn't leave quite that soon, and they understood, how about ten days?

"Ten days?" Emily repeated.

"Actually, I'm already packed," Matt said. "It's just — you know — whenever you and I — when we can — you know — "

"Say good-bye," Emily said.

"Right," Matt said.

He had sold his most precious car to buy her ring. Emily had thought she mattered more than anything else in the world. Evidently not. The prospect of lying in the dirt of Indianapolis changing tires was better.

Emily did not complain. She had not been brought up to whine and moan. She even said he could have his ring back and sell it if he needed money for the trip.

"Emily!" Matt said, shocked. "Nothing has changed. You're still my girl."

"What do you mean, nothing has changed?" she screamed at him. "You're leaving town. I'm going to be working at a florist's. Alone at night. Alone on weekends. Alone for supper. *Alone every minute.*"

"But you always liked flower arranging before," Matt protested.

"Don't you understand anything? You're leaving."

"Yes, but I still love you."

"But you're not going to be here. You'll be there."

"Well, that's where the racing team is."

They went round and round. Matt found her very confusing. So he wouldn't be here for months — so they couldn't get married and live in their own apartment — so she'd be all alone with no friends and no social life and nothing to do and nobody to love her ... so what was the big deal?

Every time Emily looked at her precious diamond ring she wanted to cry, or else did cry. Since New Year's Eve she had taken such care of her hands. A hand with a diamond ring required more hand lotion, prettier nail polish. Now the ring was cold and bright and brittle. A mindless little rock, which would outlast Matt's love for her. She hated the dumb little ring.

And her job, her lovely job, she hated that, too.

Emily had always been excited by fresh flowers. She loved to touch and smell them, arrange them, find the right ribbon for them. She loved how a person's face lit up when you delivered flowers. Nobody could accept flowers and stay mad or depressed. Flowers could soften the world.

She had been working weekends at the florist's for a year, making boutonnieres, wrist corsages, hospital bouquets, and wedding decorations. It had seemed so perfect in June, when they all graduated, and flung their caps in the air, and kissed their relatives. Matt would open a garage, she would arrange flowers, and at their wedding the following year, all their Westerly friends would come and rejoice for them.

Matt was desperate for her to be happy about his job with the racing team. "I'll call you up a lot," he would say.

"That'll be fun."

"I'll write." Matt had never even written a grocery list in his entire life.

"Great. A postcard of tires." Emily sobbed continually. Where was the lovely life she had planned? All her friends would be out of town, at college, across an ocean. Even Beth Rose would commute to new classrooms, new places to hang out new people to have a soda with. Emily would get a postcard now and then. Sit home alone with her unpleasant father watching reruns on TV.

She hadn't told any of the girls yet. What was she supposed to say to Anne, anyway? Oh, no, we won't be getting married after all, Matt likes cars better, I'll be here alone, don't worry about me, just enjoy seeing the world.

As for the party tonight, Matt could hardly wait. He would tell all the guys. "They'll be so jealous!" he said proudly to Emily. "They'll offer me bribes to let them come too. They'll say I'm the luckiest guy on earth."

On New Year's Eve, when she said she would marry him, he had called himself the luckiest guy on earth.

Emily lay on the hot slates pretending to sleep. She could not talk because her voice would crack and she'd cry. Tonight they all, even Anne, would find out that Matt was leaving her. For cars.

She slid the diamond off her finger and stared at it. Sun leaped through the prisms of the faceted jewel, sparkling with joy.

A fake, she thought. Diamonds don't feel joy. Joy was in Matt when he gave it to me, but with Matt leaving, there is no joy anywhere.

You rotten ring, Emily thought, suddenly hating it. It was the symbol of her hurt and fury and loss. Her hand trembled, holding it, and the jewel winked back a thousand times, knowing it would last longer than love.

She hated it.

Without thinking, she hurled it away, just as Matt was hurling her. It disappeared in the air and Emily covered her face with her towel, hating herself, and Matt, and the ring, and all happy people.

Chapter 6

Molly was sitting up with her head ducked forward and her towel over her hair, as if she were drying it from swimming in the pool. She wasn't. She was peering at the other girls from under the towel. The girls who had it all: Emily, Beth Rose, Kip, and Anne. The girls who had the future. While Molly had nothing.

She did not even have the right to be in Anne's yard, Anne whom she had tried to defeat for years now. But Anne was weak, and had not stopped Molly from marching in, and the others were polite and also confused, and did not kick her out, either. So Molly was with them on their last day together, when she knew they wanted privacy most of all.

She liked the idea that they could not say their sweet little good-byes because she was there. She liked how they had to sashay off through the dark, cool house and out into the front yard, because Molly had ruined the backyard for them.

Anne not only let her in, she played Little Miss Hostess, offering her cookies and Coke. "Our last box of Girl Scout cookies," she said. "Samoas. They're my favorites."

"How do you keep them so long?" Kip asked. "We order about a million boxes each year and they're gone in a week. My four brothers just look at a box of Thin Mints and they're gone."

"We freeze them," Anne said. "I hardly ever eat more than a cookie a week anyhow."

They all laughed hysterically, they who could eat a box in one sitting. "That's the diet idea I've been waiting for," Kip said. "Defrost my desserts at the rate of one cookie a week."

Molly said, "I can't believe anybody buys Girl Scout cookies. The whole Girl Scout thing is so dumb. I mean, you were never Girl Scouts, were you?" She made it sound like a socially repulsive disease.

Kip, Emily, Anne, and Beth Rose exchanged looks in the superior way of friends annoyed by a stranger. Molly hated them.

"Actually," Anne said, "I was a Brownie but never went on into Scouting."

"I did," Beth said. "I loved it. But I couldn't seem to earn any badges and after a year or so I gave up."

"That's when you know you're a loser," Molly said. "When you can't even earn a

Girl Scout badge. They give them to you just for strolling through the woods."

Anne went off to say good-bye to Beth Rose out front. Kip busied herself with a paperback. Emily slept.

Molly looked around the yard, hating it. Anne's house was so perfect, and here among the trees was a little yellow dressing house, and a big yellow awning, and cute little yellow tables, and adorable little yellow soda-fountain chairs. They even had a stack of yellow towels for the guests who went swimming.

All sunshine, that was Anne's life.

Molly dragged the towel back down over her face to hide the terrible expression of jealousy.

And Emily took off her diamond ring and threw it into the pool.

Molly continued rubbing her hair.

Impossible. Nobody would throw away their engagement ring. If they really hated the guy, they'd at least cash the ring in and have a fun time on the money. But what else tiny and glittery could she have tossed into the water?

Emily was too boring to do a wild and crazy thing like that. And surely if you decided to throw away a diamond, you'd do it when the boy was there, so he could see his hard-earned money vanish, and he could rage and be bitter and you could laugh in his face.

It shouldn't be hard to find. A nice, clean,

blue-tiled swimming pool. Provided it didn't get pulled down the drains.

If you're that mad at Matt, Molly thought, eyeing Emily from under her towel, you should have taken him down to the river's edge. Had a knock-down-drag-out, screaming fight, ripped the ring off your finger, hurled it out into the muddy water, laughed while it vanished in the swirling current, and shouted, "So there! This is what I think of you, you creep!" Now *that*, Emily old girl, would have been a scene worthy of a diamond.

It couldn't have been the ring. It was probably a prize from a Cracker Jack box or something. Molly flung herself backward onto her towel, cracking her head painfully against the slates. Neither Emily nor Kip asked if it hurt.

For Molly, high school graduation came as a complete surprise. It shouldn't have. She had taken fourth year English, was on the yearbook committee, went to the Senior Prom.

But she was completely unready for it. How could high school be over? She felt she had hardly arrived. She had barely started going to parties, laughing in the cafeteria, flirting in the halls, learning other people's locker combinations.

And it was gone.

Molly had had lots of boyfriends in her four years of high school, from simpletons like Roddy who were good for filling in the dull hours to breathtaking college guys like

Christopher with fast cars and extra money.

They were gone, too. Nobody called, nobody remembered her. It was as if not only high school had ended — Molly also had ended.

I'm seventeen, she thought, and I'm over.

She felt like a dusty black-and-white photograph, trapped on a back page in the fat yearbook. Years later somebody might flip the pages, sáying, "Who's that? I don't remember her."

After graduation, summer came hot and heavy, like thunderclouds that do not burst. It weighed Molly down. Even though her house, car, and job were air-conditioned, Molly seemed to gasp for breath all day long.

She spent her summer alone.

Over and over she thought about girls — she who had never had any use for the female sex. She who felt boys were the single answer, the only answer, the always answer.

Girls were all leaving. So what did that make Molly? A reject?

Anne came back, said nothing, and lay this time in the shade.

They all despise me, Molly thought. So big deal, I committed a few little social errors along the way. Anne committed the biggie and people gathered round in a conspiracy to pretend she was perfect anyhow. But why do I care about Anne? It's too late to be friends with her, she's leaving in less than twenty-four hours.

And I'm not interested in Kip. How could you want to spend time with the Most Academic, Most Impressive, Best Leader, and Finest Socialite all rolled into one perfect New York-bound package?

Certainly not Beth. I don't even know what Beth is doing. Beth is one of those bland people you never remember once she leaves the room, anyway.

And Emily? . . .

Molly's eyes went back to the pool.

Perhaps a last swim was called for. It would be rather nice to acquire a free diamond ring.

Chapter 7

Four girls were left.

The sun was changing colors, and collecting clouds. Purple and scarlet and gold flamed through the darkening sky. It was still hot. The breeze lifted the dusty green leaves of the trees around the pool and the evening was filled with a whispering sound.

Anne thought of her trunk, her suitcases, her flight bag, and camera. She thought of the top of her bureau, where her plane tickets and brand-new navy-blue American passport lay. Her passport photograph made her look more like a mangy little terrier than a cover girl. Her mind walked for the hundredth time over the next day's schedule. She had to get from LaGuardia Airport to the Manhattan hotel by herself and meet Ivory Glynn there. She didn't want to mess up her first solo flight. That would be terrible.

She thought of her parents and Con, indulging her little whim to go overseas, thinking she was cute. Until she pulled it off.

She thought of Ivory Glynn and film festivals, of famous stars and crowds of fans.

The sound of Molly diving into the pool startled Anne, and the lapping of water sounded like drowning. But I, too, am almost drowning, she thought. Drowning in emotion and memory and excitement.

Let me say a sweet good-bye to Con!

Let me hug all my friends without crying.

Let me not yell at my family.

Let my last summer night be perfect.

Emily's hand was hidden beneath her huge beach towel, but it felt naked, exposed, horrible. The thought of the thrown ring filled her whole head. She could hardly even remember who Anne was, or why they had to say good-bye.

Yet the anger was still there. She could not make herself go back for the ring.

Wherever it was. She had not looked. Grass, garden, pool.

It's gone, she thought miserably. Like Matt.

Oh, Matt, Matt, how could you leave me? How could you turn this into our last Saturday night together?

Kip yanked on her jeans and white shirt. I have to get rid of Molly for Anne, she thought. I can pretend we're going somewhere, give Molly the wrong directions, and then we'll rush like mad toward the river and vanish.

Not very nice, but then, Molly is not very nice. You reap what you sow. She wants to be nasty her whole seventeen years, she gets a nasty harvest, that's all.

It was Kip who had done most of the work for the party. Oh, Con paid the bills, but he kept calling Kip up and wheedling her into making the arrangements for him. First it was rent the boat for him, and then it was find a little band for him, and then arrange fireworks for him. Finally get a caterer for him. "You're so clever at this," he would tell Kip. "You know the ins and outs, everything you touch turns out perfectly."

"Get lost, Con."

"But it's for Anne, not me. Please, Kippie?"

Her little brother called her Kippie. She hated it. When she went to college she would dumb that stupid nickname forever and be Katharine. She imagined a slew of handsome boys calling Katharine, Katharine! She would turn gracefully on those crowded New York streets and smile back at them. Hi, Tod. Hi, Bob. Hi, Kenny.

Con was so handsome. Every time he begged, Kip gave in. Those intense eyes and flickering smiles had been winning the girls since grammar school.

Molly's brittle, demanding whine broke into her thoughts. "Come on, guys let's go some-place air-conditioned and have a great time."

"There's a new juice bar on Michigan Avenue," Kip suggested teasingly.

"Oh, Kip, don't be weird. A juice bar? Get a life. Why would we want to go to a juice bar? How about the movies?"

"That's a thought," Kip said. She found her purse and car keys. "I'll give you a ride home, Molly. Anne has to finish packing. Emily, you need a ride home?"

Anne got misty. "Oh, Kip, this is *it*. This is good-*bye*. I'm actually *leaving*. So are *you*."

"You sound like a drum roll," Kip teased her.

They flung their arms around each other.

"Oh, Kippie, do you think it'll all work out?" cried Anne, as if her parents' lack of faith had suddenly penetrated. How cruel parents can be, Kip thought. Raise a child for eighteen years and then tell her she isn't ready.

"You'll be perfect," Kip said softly. They hugged fiercely. "Don't send me postcards," Kip said. "I want you to be so busy and having so much fun you never get to a post office."

They hugged again. The tears that came were real, and painful. It was not a sham good-bye, a false good-bye that had worried Kip, since they would do it all over again in a few hours. It was real and it hurt.

Anne kept standing by Kip's car, crying, "Oh, we should have planned something special!"

Emily said, weeping, "Yes, this is terrible."

Molly added, "It's not too late; let's all do something later on."

I'll have to drive over her foot to shut her up, Kip thought. This was so attractive she almost did it. Exercising control, she said, "Just get in the car, will you, Molly?"

Kip drove away, one hand on the wheel, one hand waving to Anne, and Emily passed her a Kleenex for her tears.

Kip began to get excited. There was nothing like a party. Especially a party on the *Duet* — a river cruise — dancing by the moonlight out on the water!

Oh, what a Saturday night!

Molly just stood there during the sickening little good-byes Emily and Kip said to Anne, with little cries of pain and loss, as if they would sob every night missing old Anne.

She got in the backseat of Kip's huge station wagon, among the debris of four little brothers.

They'll all go somewhere, Molly Nelmes thought. I'll be here doing nothing. Dwindling away.

She was afraid.

The days stretched out in front, empty and useless. School was bad, but filled the days with boys and action. Even long summers came to an end. Not this year. Now there were neither endings nor beginnings.

Molly looked down at the little object she had rescued from the bottom of the pool.

Action, she thought. Either I find it . . . or I make it.

Chapter 8

All of Anne Stephens' house was lovely, but
the staircase was superb. It turned twice
inside the large, open hall, each landing
carpeted with a small Oriental rug in vivid
reds and blues. Pale wooden bannisters
gleamed under the sunshine pouring in
through the skylights.

From the time she was a toddler, Anne had
been taught to make an "entrance" on those
stairs. Her parents were camera addicts.
They had pictures of Anne posing on the
higher landing in her new Snoopy pajamas
— age three — Christmas Eve. Pictures of
Anne in her princess costume — age seven —
Halloween. Pictures of Anne dressed for
tennis or dances or the movies — age thirteen
to eighteen — going out with Con Winter.

There was no sun tonight, only the soft
dimmed lights recessed in the vaulted ceilings.
Anne made her last grand entrance and her

parents, as always, stood at the bottom of the stairs, cameras ready.

Who looks at all those photographs? Anne thought. Not me. I've never opened a single album. She wondered if while she was gone her parents would sit together on the sofa and turn the pages of the albums, staring at the daughter who was grown and gone. It was a sad, rainy day thought.

Con stood where he always stood, a few feet inside the front door, ready for a quick exit, head cocked to the side, eyes fastened on the spot where she would first appear.

Anne knew her own beauty. But she often forgot Con's. He had a fluid, dark handsomeness, unexpressive as a statue. He was simply there, resting, for you to admire. His eyes were heavy-lidded, sleepy, and his hair thick and softly falling, so that Anne's continual impulse was to sweep it from his eyes. She remembered in Ancient History staring at the photograph of the sculpture "Apollo Belvedere" and thinking — *it's Con*.

She paused on the landing from long habit. Her thin, gauzy Indian dress hung like a blue cloud, its narrow fringe of embroidery like jewels below her throat. She had left her hair down, and the golden silk of it slid over her shoulders.

Anne never saw Con without falling in love with him all over again. Don't let it happen tonight! she thought, trying not to see how he needed a haircut again, how he looked tired, how he must want comfort.

"You look beautiful," Con said, in that husky voice of his, as if he were filled with emotion. Experience told Anne that it was not emotion, it was just that Con had a husky voice. But she could not resist him and went straight to him, sliding the hair off his forehead and leaving her fingers momentarily caught in his hair. Her mother snapped a picture. Anne swallowed and looked away from him. "Where are we going?" she asked.

He linked his arm through hers. "Dinner." He smiled at her. They were exactly the same height, and their eyes always met. For years, Anne had thought this meant they were on the same emotional and mental wavelength.

Con wrapped a lock of her hair around his own finger and drew it in a golden mustache above his lips. "I love your hair down," he said.

Con was good at compliments. Anne's mother and his own mother had been teaching him. It did not come naturally. Anne was very touched. She knew he had rehearsed what to say. Because I matter to him, she thought. *Oh, I am going to miss Con so much!*

They walked out of the house. Con had been allowed to borrow his father's new convertible. Anne clapped her hands with delight. She ran back in to get a scarf to tie over her hair to keep it from getting too tangled, and they drove off, Con going fast, the breeze pulling at them, and the blaring radio audible only when they stopped at corners. He tossed her a grin, grabbed her hand, and kissed it quick before putting his hand back on the wheel.

Her heart was tossed back in his lap.

For the first time she wondered what she was doing — abandoning everything that was love, that was friendship?

I am traveling to strange cities with an old lady when Con loves me and wants me here, she thought. Maybe — maybe —

She wrenched her mind off it. She had to look away from Con in order to think of other things. It was going to be a long dinner, if she had to keep from looking his way throughout the meal.

Molly had slowly gotten out of Kip's car. It was not air-conditioned and she was hot and sticky from the plastic upholstery. Kip was aflame with her own thoughts, bright and eager for something. College, probably, thought Molly sourly, hating Kip for having something to look forward to.

Kip had a hard time pulling back into traffic. The car windows were all down for air. Molly was only a few feet away on her own front yard when Emily said clearly, "So what time are we all supposed to get there?"

Kip ripped out into the street, motor roaring, taking chances with an oncoming truck, but sick of waiting. That was Kip for you.

So there *is* action, Molly thought. And *all* of them are part of it.

She flew inside, yelled to her stepfather, "I have to borrow the car!" and grabbed his keys from the kitchen counter where they were always tossed. She glanced down at what she had on. A very short, bright red skirt, a man's shirt that was longer than the skirt, made flouncy in the middle by a huge metal glittering belt. Only a few weeks before Molly had gotten a very short geometric haircut, so fixing her hair was a thing of the past. Nothing could change it. She had makeup in her handbag.

Molly ran right out of the house and drove even faster than Kip, catching her two traffic lights down. They both sat at the red. Molly slid her newest piece of jewelry on one finger. Maybe I should flash it at Emily, she thought. Even better, flash it at Matt. Wonder if they'll recognize it? That would add to the fun all around, wouldn't it?

Molly laughed.

Chapter 9

A quarter mile downriver from the *Duet*'s
dock was a hill and a tourist overlook. It was
one of Emily's favorite views and Matt
routinely pulled in so they could look across
the blue water at the bluff, the trees, and the
white houses on the far shore. Tonight he
almost skipped it because he was so upset
with her, but decided that this night of all
nights, he had better pause at the tourist
overlook. Whatever few traditions he and
Emily had, Matt knew he should try to cele-
brate right up to the moment of departure.

So Matt parked the car, and as he set the
brake he thought of the cars he would work
on shortly, and the team and the things he
would learn, and his heart soared. He got
out smiling and circled the car to open the
door for Emily. He took her hand in his,
wishing she could be as thrilled about the job
as he was. It blunted all his pleasure to deal
with Emily's anger. Her hand was — her
hand —

"Emily!" Matt said. "Where — your ring — how come — where is it?"

She did not look his way. Her face was set in anger and she stared across the river. "It didn't matter to me anymore."

He could not believe what she had said. He held her hand up to the light, like a banker checking for counterfeit money. "It matters to me!" Matt said. "I still love you. Just because I'm taking a better job doesn't mean I can't still love you."

She turned a second time, this time facing the road. Matt hated it when she wouldn't look into his eyes. He took her arms and held her firmly, but he should have known better. "Pushing me around now?" said Emily through gritted teeth.

"Okay, okay, I'm sorry, stand any way you like. What did you do with my ring? Stick it in your jewelry box? Leave it on your desk? Emily, it's not some dumb pair of cheap earrings from a carnival. I sold a whole car to buy that ring for you."

"You should have found out about your job with the racing team before you wasted your money," Emily snapped.

He didn't know what to make of her. Why was it impossible to do two thing at once? Why couldn't he stay in love with her *and* join the pit crew? "Emily," he said for the hundredth time, "so a few months go by and I'm not around. It doesn't mean I'm going to date other girls, or not come back. It means I'm going to learn a fabulous trade and earn a lot of money and —" he broke it off just in time. He had almost said, "And have a lot of fun." He knew the response to *that* statement. Emily would demand to know what kind of fun he expected *her* to have, stuck in Westerly without him.

But she could hardly come along. They would be on the move, so she wouldn't be able to earn money to help. His salary wouldn't keep them in motels. She had to stay and eventually he'd come home. It seemed to Matt this was straight and reasonable. He could not believe they were arguing about it yet again.

And he had been looking forward to this party so much. They all needed a final summer night: a good-bye not just for Anne, but for all of them. And he, too, needed an audience — people who would rejoice for him, who would clap him on the back, and in whose eyes he would see envy.

"I want you to wear the ring," he said finally. He tried to kiss her but she moved toward the car. "Can we drive back to your house and get it, Em?"

"No."

"Why not? Please wear it. For me."

"No."

"Why not?" He was yelling now. People in other cars looked their direction.

"Because I threw it away. It doesn't exist anymore. It wasn't worth anything to me. So there, Matthew O'Connor. You're not the only person who can throw things away."

Kip's brothers ranged in age from six to sixteen. Their appetites were unbelievable. You no sooner filled the station wagon to the brim with food and unloaded it all over the kitchen, so that every shelf and cabinet was overflowing, then the boys had finished it and were complaining of hunger.

Both parents worked, and all five children had definite chores. Kip was the grocery shopper. George was head cook. She decided on hot dogs, cole slaw, baked potatoes, milk (the boys drank gallons each day), fried apples, and mint chocolate-chip ice cream. Nobody could complain about that. George disliked shredding cabbage, so, feeling kind, Kip bought a bag of pre-shredded.

She kept glancing over her shoulder. It was very strange, but she had a feeling that Molly had followed her here to the grocery. You knew you watched too much television when you began thinking things like that.

She had dropped Molly off first. Then she and Emily drove on to Em's, with Emily oddly silent, gripping her towel like a life raft. "You okay, Em?" Kip had asked.

"Sure. Fine. Heat got to me." Emily got out of Kip's car and Kip drove quickly away to complete her family chores, get home, get changed, and reach the docks in time to organize the party for Con. She had promised to get everybody well hidden, so Anne would suspect nothing when she strolled along the river for a last view of Westerly.

Kip got in what looked like the quickest checkout line and which, of course, turned out to be the slowest. When she was finally through, she pushed her cart of brown paper bags out into the parking lots, her eyes flickering over the other cars, looking for Molly.

This is ridiculous, Kip thought. What would Molly follow me for?

She saw herself driving madly through unknown alleys, whipping down dark lanes, following narrow twisting streets, trying to throw Molly off.

Of course, Westerly was laid out on a grid without a single twist or alley, so it was an unlikely chase.

Kip was so annoyed with herself she refused to look in her rearview mirror the rest of the way home, lest she pretend it was Molly she saw behind her.

The party was Con's mother's idea. Con would never have thought of it himself, and once his mother mentioned it, Con wanted to ignore her. "I don't want to give her a party," Con protested. "I'm so mad at her, I'd rather — "

Well, he could hardly tell his own mother

he would rather kill Anne than give her a party. He turned his back on his mother instead and stared out through a broken window into a side yard. They had been in this latest house only ten days, and remodeling had hardly begun. Anne had not been here yet. Now she never would. At the rate Con's mother bought, fixed up, and sold at a profit the old Victorian houses that were scattered around the city of Westerly, the Winters would be living in yet another one by the time Anne returned from seeing the world.

If Anne returned.

If she could be bothered to telephone Con once she did.

"Now, now. You two have been dating steadily since you were in junior high," Con's mother said. She put aside the memory of the days when they dated others or the long, sad stretch when Anne was (as the four parents referred to it) Out Of Town.

"That's right," said Con huffily, "and Anne shouldn't be dumping me like this. And if she is, she should at least ask me first before she goes and gets a job instead of coming with me to school."

"I don't know how I raised a son like you," said his mother, laughing. "A girl doesn't need your permission to arrange her adult life, any more than you need hers."

Con sulked. He was good at this. Usually Anne rose to the occasion, trying to sweep away his bad humor as if her task in life was to keep Con happy. This was a pleasant contrast to Con's mother, who felt that if her son wanted to be in a bad mood, that was his problem, not hers. Anne would rush forward, offering distraction, comfort, affection, and homemade brownies.

Con liked being with Anne. She was invariably the loveliest girl in any gathering, and boys and men admired Con for having Anne as much as they admired Anne for looking the way she did.

But it was the end of summer. Anne was about to possess the world and he would be an ordinary freshman on a campus with nearly twenty thousand other students. He would have to fight for a place like anybody else, and hunt for pretty girls, and struggle for grades. At State, he would be nobody.

The whole thing was an outrage. If Anne just did as she was told, and went with him, he could continue college just as if it were high school.

Con's mother went right out and rented the *Duet*.

Rather than exert himself, Con sweet-talked Kip into making every other arrangement. Old Beth Rose agreed to run the dumber errands.

Con had a sudden insight.

With Anne no longer shining by his side, he, Con, would be the boring one. Like Beth, good for the dumber errands.

His resentment at being left behind filled his chest. Some party it would be.

And he'd have to act all night as if he were enjoying it.

Matthew O'Connor remembered once in soccer when he was knocked down so hard that hitting the ground whacked all the air out of his lungs. It was a strange, collapsed, deathlike feeling. No air. No strength. He remembered how the coach's face swam above him and the air seemed thick like cloth and would not enter his lungs and revive him. "Is he hurt?" everybody had shouted. "Nah," shouted the coach back, "just has to catch a breath."

Matt stared at Emily, and struggled once more to catch a breath. She was so mad at him she had actually thrown away his ring? Like the paper wrapping of a Big Mac?

Her features were small and old-fashioned. He always thought of her as a heroine in a silent movie. It did not surprise him when she stalked off, got back into the car, and slammed the door.

He loved her.

He did not know what to do. The whole situation was like a math equation that would not work to a solution. It should be so simple. Boy goes to job, girl waits.

Matt got into the car with her. He was actually afraid to touch her, for fear that along with throwing his ring away, she would throw him away.

He drove mechanically to the dock.

How were they supposed to get through a party now?

Kip rushed through her schedule. She and the boys unpacked the groceries. George accepted her menu, and especially the pre-shredded cabbage, with delight. She hopped into the shower to rinse the chlorine out of her hair. She blew it dry, put on her dress, slid her bare feet into her sandals, and left.

Kip loved bare feet. That was the most wonderful thing about summer. Freedom of the foot.

Briefly Kip wondered if Mike would be at the party. He had been her first real boyfriend, and they had drifted apart, never quite becoming ordinary friends again. She really regretted this, but it happened to everybody else, too. If only when you stopped seeing a boy, you could still be buddies. She really liked Mike. It would be nice to be able to chat with him as easily as with anybody else. Maybe it would happen tonight.

She drove to the parking lot by the river and got out of her car. "Hey, Kippie!" shouted some of the kids already there. "*Now* the party will start! Kip's aboard!"

Kip laughed with delight and danced up the gangplank onto the *Duet*.

Chapter 10

Beth Rose had a favorite, unnamed daydream. She played it continually and never tired of it. It was a game in which the Perfect Boy would show up at last, just around the next corner. It was a daydream never fulfilled, and yet always hopeful. By the end of a typical day Beth would have dreamed up at least a dozen situations in which this Perfect Boy could show up, but never did.

When she drove away from Anne's, she headed for the difficult intersection at Fifth and Maple. She would have to stop at the red light there, wait through two or three light changes as she crawled through the summer traffic. This would surely be the day when a convertible — a red one — driven by a terrific handsome teenage boy — would pull up next to her — perhaps with a second terrific handsome boy in the passenger seat. Beth Rose would toss her auburn curls and wink at them. The passenger would be so attracted to her, he'd vault out of the convertible, not even pausing to open the door, and race around her car as the traffic ground to a halt and horns honked. He'd leap into *her* passenger seat, and kiss her, and Beth Rose would have found true love.

However, she arrived at the traffic light at Fifth and Maple and next to her was a station wagon driven by a grim-looking mother whose toddlers were invisible inside their white crash seats. The passenger side was entirely full of brown paper bags and groceries.

Beth discarded that dream and planned that when she drove up her own street, the house two down from hers would finally have been sold, and the family moving in would have a perfect teenage boy. Oh, heck, make it good. *Three* perfect teenage boys. They'd all be in love with her. Probably fight over her.

However, the FOR SALE sign was still imbedded in the grass.

Beth went on into her own house, dark and cool, to shower and change for the party. Into a carryall she slipped white jeans, an XXL sweatshirt that said HARD ROCK CAFE NEW YORK, and her bathing suit. She slid into her dress. It was pale lemon-yellow, sprinkled with confetti dots of white that were almost invisible. The skirt was tulip-shaped with lettuce ruffles. The dress was sleeveless, cool and comfortable, and in the wind the skirt filled and swirled and made her feel wonderfully feminine.

Beth was slim but the heavy yellow belt made her look positively skinny. She loved that. Her mother didn't. Her mother said she Looked Like Death, and When Was She Going To Eat More? and did Beth want to read this little pamphlet on Anorexia?

Mother, Beth would say, I am not too thin, I love food, I eat enough. They would eye each other suspiciously and drop the conversation.

Beth thought forlornly about Gary. She would probably never be over her crush on Gary. Carry it to her grave, no doubt. When she was an old crone of eighty-six she would be sick and delirious, still muttering the name Gary. By then she wouldn't have had a date with him in seven decades.

Gary would be at the party tonight, of course; he was a good friend of Con's and always appeared at any party.

She and Gary had dated on and off for a year. Gary was drifty. Half aware of the world, not of the world. For Gary, graduation had been the end of torture known as school. Gary was already at work in his father's restaurant, his adult life in place, and Gary was evidently pleased.

Doesn't he want anything different? Beth thought.

But Gary didn't want anything at all, as

far as Beth could tell. Days and nights circled round him, and he enjoyed himself and that was his world. Whereas Beth was filled with desperate yearnings and overpowering hopes. "Like what?" Gary used to ask her.

"Don't you want adventure?" she would cry. "New places? Different thoughts? New everything, from clothing to telephone numbers? More worlds?"

Gary wanted a new car. He couldn't think of anything else he'd replace.

Beth fixed her hair, setting the impossibly thick red locks in hot rollers, hoping it would keep the planned wave through the evening, but knowing it wouldn't because of the humidity out on the river. She had let it get very long, and because it was so thick, it just stuck out, like a horse's mane in the wind. Sometimes Beth loved her hair, and other times she could not believe she actually appeared in public with that tangled mass of hair flying in people's faces.

She laced on her sandals — white, with soles so thin she'd be lucky if they lasted the whole night. She didn't like them after all and ran around trying to find a different pair. "Beth!" shrieked her mother. "Just go. I can't stand it, you look perfect, now leave!"

So she went.

"Put air in those tires!" shouted her father as she drove off. "They're too low."

She detoured to the garage. Maybe to replace that repulsive guy with the missing teeth, some adorable college boy would have been hired to pump gas, and. . . .

There wasn't anybody to pump gas. She had to put air in the tires herself, holding her skirt carefully off the greasy pavement with one hand and trying to get the cap off the tire valve with two fingers so she wouldn't get oil all over her hands.

When that was done, she ran into traffic leaving the shopping center. She inched miserably along in the heat. You'd think with a million cars, *one* of them would be full of teenage boys. But you'd be wrong, Beth thought. Teenage boys do not go to the mall on Saturday afternoon.

Finally she got to Benjie's. No handsome boy served her. Two middle-aged women, whose weight indicated they ate entire boxes of the rich, homemade ice cream all day, handed her Con's order. Beth Rose resolved to have only a tiny taste of ice cream, lest she grow up to resemble these creatures. "You got a cooler?" asked one fat woman.

"A cooler?" Beth said.

They looked at her as if they didn't sell ice cream to people as dumb as her. Ninety degrees and a long, slow drive to Westerly River. "No," said Beth in a small voice.

"Better drive fast," they told her.

But there was no way to drive medium, let alone fast. Traffic filled the roads. Ahead of Beth a car stalled in the heat and had to be pushed onto the shoulder. The ice cream began to melt.

Great, thought Beth. People who want ice cream will have to get in my car and lick it off the upholstery.

She had forgotten to put on her watch. A thin band of pale skin on her wrist showed where it ought to be. Instead it was lying in the bathroom on the shelf. She put the radio on. All her favorite songs got played but nobody mentioned the time. Her right ankle began hurting from being in first gear for so long. The speedometer never went above fifteen.

At last she neared the river and prepared to make the tricky turn across traffic to the dock parking lots. She could see kids on board the *Duet*, distant bright shirts and skirts, mingling like flowers in a vase.

The parking lot was full. She circled the lot a second time. I don't believe this, Beth thought. What I want in life is romance and what I get is low tires, stalled cars, and full lots.

The *Duet* began pulling away from the dock.

Beth jumped out of the car. "No, no, wait! I have the ice cream! You can't leave without me!"

"Lady," shouted the driver behind her, "you're blocking traffic. Get back in and drive."

She got in and drove desperately, finally pulling right up on the grass, crumpling the NO PARKING ON THE GRASS sign. The *Duet* pulled remorselessly away from the shore. She ripped open the door to carry her ice cream.

"You can't park here," said a policeman.

"I know, but I have the ice cream," Beth said miserably, "and the boat —"

"Is gone," said the policeman sympathetically. "Now drive back across the main road and park in the commuter lot. You'll have to hire a boat to catch up to them, if you really want them to have that ice cream." He looked in the backseat. "Not that anybody will want it now."

There was no choice. She obeyed, parked across the road, and staggered across the stopped traffic with an armload of melting ice cream.

The *Duet* was too far out in the river even to yell at.

This is my life, thought Beth Rose. This is my entrance to adulthood. Kip goes to New York. Anne sees the world. Emily gets married. I sit on the dock with ice cream melting around my ankles.

I have truly missed the boat.

Chapter 11

Jeremiah Dunstan shouldered the heavy movie camera and waited for the white convertible to appear. He had shot the arrival of each party guest and had a nice scene of them crouched down in various corners in the little boat. He was hot and tired and wished he could be a guest instead of a hired hand.

Back last summer Jere and his father had taken (as they always did) day trips downriver with people who wanted to fish. They were mostly working men who could fit only a couple days of fishing into their lives each year. They wanted action. Unfortunately, fishing on the Westerly River was not a high-action item.

Jere had been given a movie camera for his birthday, because at the time he insisted he would be a famous Hollywood director. It had turned out to be more work and less fun and a lot more expense than he had bargained for. Plus, who did you show these films to? You needed an awfully kind girlfriend and Jere hadn't found one.

Then on one of the fishing trips, Jere brought the movie camera along. He was hoping to get good river shots for a film he wanted to make about a runaway kid. The client of the day, who had caught a small insignificant fish, shouted, "Film me! Film me!" He spent the rest of the trip focusing in on Mr. Stein reeling in, Mr. Falkland eating another roast beef on rye, Mr. Swanzey pretending to dive over the side. At the end of the day, they asked Jere if they could buy the film.

Jere was off and running. He advertised in four local papers and circulars, and had more work that summer than he could handle. Everybody wanted a movie of their wedding, Fourth of July party, or first baby's christening.

Jere was a year younger than most of the guests at the party on the *Duet*. They had graduated in June and he still had his senior year to go. Since Westerly was a huge high school, he knew this crowd only by sight and they did not know him at all.

He hoisted the camera for the next quartet of guests. They would be immortalized together.

Molly parked next to adorable old Gary, who dated every girl once and hardly any girl twice. Only Beth Rose. Molly had never figured that one out. She had a feeling even Gary had never figured that one out. "Hi, Gary," she said sweetly.

"Hey, Moll, how ya doin', how's summer been?" Gary sauntered on toward the dock. Molly fell in step with him.

Mike (Kip's old boyfriend) and Toby (nobody's boyfriend ever, so far) hopped out of a car to join them. Nobody mentioned that it was odd for Molly to be part of this particular gathering; only girls would think of that. Boys were so nice and thick, thought Molly contentedly. You could count on a boy never to spot the things that mattered.

She hooked her arm through Gary's. Gary was pretty hard to surprise. He looked down at her arm and laughed, and when the kid with the movie camera focused on them, Gary lifted their two arms to wave. Molly pirouetted for the camera and lost Gary in the process; Gary always kept going, kind of like a tank; either you kept up or you got lost or crushed.

Kip was busy organizing the pile of goodbye presents out of sight, so that the gift wrap and ribbons wouldn't glitter in Anne's eyes and give it all away. Molly felt grateful that she was nothing at all like Kip Elliott.

"Okay, now everybody has to hide!" shouted Kip in her General-with-the-Troops voice. "There's the cabin, the life-preserver cabinets, the benches. I want everybody to find a place and I'll stand out on the dock and inspect."

Inspect! Molly thought, laughing at her. Only Kip would make a party have an inspection. The girl is pitiful.

"Don't you like it how Kip always has things under control?" Gary asked. "Nothing ever goes wrong if Kip is running it."

Molly said to him very seriously, as if she really wanted to know the answer, "Why don't you date Kip, Gary?" Boys always fell for that tone of voice and gave her honest answers. Girls were harder to fool.

"I'd date Kip all right," Gary said, "but I don't think Kip would date me. She wants the world. All I ever want is the next dance."

Molly laughed and so did Gary. She thought, now *there's* a possibility. I'd take Gary in a heartbeat. And maybe tonight, I will!

"Quiet!" Kip thundered from somewhere out on the dock. "No more whispering, no more laughing. I want utter and complete silence."

Molly giggled. "Honestly, she is so —"

'Sssssssh!" hissed everybody else.

Molly sank back in her dark corner to sulk. But she came out of it quickly. She had gotten on board. And this was one party where they couldn't make a crasher leave. There was going to be a whole river between Molly and her car.

* * *

Con drove to the river. He and Anne had parked there many an evening, winter and summer, staring at the water, staring at each other, hearts beating hard, words impossible to find, but action easy to come by.

Anne was afraid to look at him. She was swamped by her memories. Strange how the terrible moments became good when looking back, simply because they had been shared. They were part of the whole existence of Con and Anne as a pair, that had turned them into the two individuals they were now.

Anne wet her lips. She was beginning to melt. Not from the heat. From Con.

The *Duet* was docked, quietly rocking in the river awaiting its next journey. Its dark green paint gleamed, and the setting sun flickered tongues of gold across the gilt paint and brass fitting.

"*Duet*," whispered Con. "We were one once."

Her eyes filled with tears.

"I guess you're a solo now," he said lightly. But when she turned to look at him, a muscle in his jaw was twitching with tension.

"Dinner reservations aren't for a while," Con said, suddenly getting out of the car. "Come on. We've got time. Let's just sit on the deck benches for a few minutes." He took her hand and did not circle the convertible to open the door for her, but drew her to her feet and lifted her over the steering wheel and door. She laughed with delight. The wind caught her blue dress and lifted it like a balloon, and let it down again just as Con let her down.

Jere hoisted his camera as the white convertible drew up. He stood next to his father's plain, unremarkable van, effectively camouflaged just by being too dull next to the glittering boat and the river in the sun.

The boy was Con Winter, greatly admired at Westerly High, definitely a big man on campus. Jere didn't think much of the breed. Too pretty for his taste, too aware of themselves.

And with him, of course, Anne Stephens.

Jere loved photographing her. In her slender, cool, golden way she was so lovely. She moved with grace, slowly, as if concentrating on each step. Definitely a person who looked before she leaped. He slipped around his truck and knelt beside a large green trash barrel at the water's edge. He got a wonderful picture of Anne, close-up, dreamily looking out beyond the boat, toward the horizon.

She turned to Con, and they kissed, very lightly, and he caught it perfectly; they were silhouetted against the purple streaked sky and the wind was lifting her hair.

But it did not seem real to Jere. The couple was too lovely. They actually looked made for movies, and not for real life. He felt no envy for them, only delight that he could be the cameraman.

He swiveled to face the deck, ready for the burst of kids.

Anne had celebrated her seventh birthday on the *Duet*. She remembered her friends' excitement. How everybody had Dixie cups of ice cream and wanted to throw the cups overboard when they had eaten, and pretend they were flotillas of boats, and have races with them. The captain said No, very sternly, it was Pollution. For years Anne thought pollution was something Dixie cups did.

She walked up the gangplank, which was a wide gray slab with narrow chain rails, dangling like iron ribbons. It seemed odd that there was nobody about to take tickets. Probably it had been rented for a private party and she and Con should not just —

"SURPRISE!" screamed fifty voices.

From every cabinway and door, from behind every bench and below each solid rail, leaped every single friend she had. Emily and Matt and Kip and Gary and Mike and Peter and Jody and Susan and Lynda and Jimmy —

"SURPRISE!"

"Happy good-bye party!"

"Bon voyage!"

"Good luck!"

"Sharon, that's a dumb thing to say, you can't have a *happy* good-bye party."

"We're not sad for her, are we?"

"No, we're jealous of her! We get to say good-bye to our parents and she gets to say good-bye to the United States!"

"You wouldn't get me to do it. All it is is sleeping in strange beds with different radio stations and getting jet lag and eating crummy hotel food and not understanding the languages. Ugh. You couldn't pay me to go."

"You could pay *me* to go! Please, please, somebody pay *me* to go!"

They had brought little gifts. Nothing big, they didn't have the money and Anne didn't have the suitcase space. Writing paper, a money belt, a pencil that said WESTERLY HIGH. Toby had heard there was terrible purse snatching in Rome so he gave her a can of Mace. Susan was afraid she would forget her own country, so she had xeroxed a copy of the Declaration of Independence. From Gary came two miniature American flags. "You be sure to wave them if you stumble into any anti-American demonstrations," he told her.

Con was quite indignant. " If she stumbles into any anti-American demonstrations, she's to *leave*, not draw attention to herself!" he said. "You think I want my girl hurt?"

Anne's eyes blurred and spilled over.

Oh, Con, Con! You sweet, loving boy. You did all this for me! You care so much!

Anne turned in the press of hugs and friends to find Con. He was standing on top of a deck bench, one foot on the seat, one knee bent and that foot on the backrest. The wind blew his shirt into a hundred folds and his hair waved like the flags. Those dark wonderful eyes seemed open only for Anne. He kissed the air. She kissed it back. They caught each other's kisses.

I can't go after all, Anne thought. Leave this? This is what life is all about — love and friends.

Chapter 12

They forgot me, Beth Rose Chapman thought. They didn't even notice that I'm not on board. I suppose the moment Anne and Con got there, they started the engines and raised the anchor.

The vanishing *Duet* gleamed once more at the bend in the river, as if winking cruelly.

"At least," said a friendly voice, "you have plenty of ice cream to eat."

Beth turned. She was a girl who cried easily, but right now there were no tears. It was too awful for tears. She felt completely desolate. Her last good-bye, and she would never make it. The final summer night, and she was not part of it. And nobody noticed.

"Can't be that bad," said the boy who was facing her. The sun was right in his eyes and he wrinkled up his entire face against the rays, even his mouth and cheeks. Beth shifted position so he could see her without squinting. Why am I always the thoughtful one, she asked herself, but nobody is thoughtful back to me?

"I'll miss the party," she said dolefully.

The sun chose that moment to disappear. The glittering river went black, the hot breeze turned damp and chilly, and the river lay empty.

"Important party?" the boy asked.

She nodded. Her throat hurt.

"You want me to rent us a boat and I'll catch you up to them?" he asked her.

Beth stared. "How clever of you!" Beth cried. "That would be wonderful. Where do we rent a boat? Yes, of course!"

He laughed and picked up half the ice cream. "You live in this town?"

"All my life."

"And you don't know where to rent a boat?"

"I've always gone on the *Duet*, if I've gone at all."

The kid shook his head, as if he had come to expect that sort of idiocy from Westerly natives. Beth scooped up her share of the ice cream and walked in step with him. He was tall and thin, wearing cutoff jeans and no shirt. The shirt he had tied around his waist. It fluttered out behind. Around his neck was a single, thick, flat, gold chain and his dark hair was rather long and kept catching in the chain. She wondered if it bothered him. It would drive her crazy.

He was very tan. Probably hadn't worn a shirt since June.

They arrived at the boat rentals. "Yep, I'm the guy," a big bearded man assured them. He grinned from under coils of scrubby gray hair and beard. "Had this boat just waiting for you two."

He made it sound like a date. Beth was a little taken aback by how small the boats were — little bitty dinghies, which looked very tippable. "I'm not a great swimmer," she said nervously.

The boy was insulted. "I'm not going to require you to swim," he said with dignity. "I am going to deliver you to your boat happy and dry." He glanced at her. "Although maybe a bit sticky with ice cream."

The boatman — "Calvin" was embroidered on the pocket of his workshirt — helped her into the skiff and she sat gingerly, right in the center, worried about breathing too hard and dumping them in the water. Calvin would certainly have the laugh of the day if that happened.

The boy jumped in, the boat swayed, the ice cream rolled around, and he sat down hard next to the engine. It had a rip cord which was very hard to pull, and when pulled, accomplished nothing. On the eighth try, with terrific effort, he got the engine going. Calvin was grinning from ear to ear on his deck, feet splayed apart, as if he purposely designed his engines to start no sooner than the eighth try. He winked at Beth Rose. The man had to be sixty, and he was irresistably cute standing there half laughing at her. Beth winked back and they both laughed.

The little skiff shot out into the marina, swerving past the rows of docked boats, and avoiding the incoming motorboats. When they were free of the water traffic and out in the middle of the river, the boy turned to smile at her.

It's him, Beth Rose thought. This is the corner. I turned it and didn't even notice him there.

The boy's mouth in repose was slightly open, as if he were about to speak or laugh. His face was no longer wrinkled in the sun, but long and thin, with thin features, as if he were a person of sharp edges and hidden thoughts. "We knights in shining armor always get our engines going in the end," he told Beth.

She began to feel that missing the party on the *Duet* was going to have it advantages. A night on the river with this boy would be a wonderful ending to the summer.

She thought about that. It was more likely to be a wonderful *beginning* to the autumn. "What's your name?" she said, eager for details. "You're not from Westerly? Where do you go to high school? Are you here for the summer? Did you just move here?"

"Pick one," he shouted over the roaring engine, "and maybe I'll tell you."

"Name," Beth yelled back.

"Blaze."

"Really?"

"Really. My parents are trendy."

"I like it."

She forgot to be nervous and leaned way forward to catch his words better. "Where from?" she yelled.

"Arizona."

"What are you doing a thousand miles from home?"

"You ever take geography? You have any idea where Arizona is? It's an awful lot more than a thousand miles."

"Beth Rose," she shouted.

"Beth did what?"

"No, no, not Beth stood up, Beth Rose, that's my name, Beth Rose."

He cut the motor during her speech. Her last two words resounded across the entire river. People on shore glanced over at them and Blaze laughed at her. "Beth Rose" seemed to echo all around them.

Beth blushed. "Would you like to drink some blueberry ice cream, Blaze? It's homemade. The very best."

He picked up an entire gallon and peeled off the cardboard lid. "Don't mind if I do, Miss Beth Rose." He drank deep from the blueberry ice cream and wiped his mouth with the back of his hand. This seemed incredibly funny to Beth and she took the gallon from him and had a swig herself. "That's disgusting," she said. "I never drank blueberry ice cream before."

"I'll have your share. I liked it."

"What are you doing here, instead of being safely in Arizona?"

"Having the most boring summer of my entire life."

They were sitting knee to knee now. She could stop shouting and didn't have to lean close to hear, but she stayed close anyhow. "There's nothing worse than being bored," she sympathized. "Especially for a whole summer. You have to come to our party. You'll meet everybody. We're mostly just-graduated seniors. Are you? It's bad timing, because this is the last Saturday of summer. But at least you can have one night that's not boring."

"I'd like that," the boy said. He nodded several times and took hold of the rip cord to start the motor again. Nothing happened. Not the second, not the third try. By the tenth he was gleaming with sweat. She wished she were a good swimmer. She would suggest a dive into the water for both of them.

Blaze said ruefully, "I don't think we're going to catch up to the *Duet* very soon."

Beth could think of worse fates. "Well, here. Try drinking chocolate. That might go down even better than blueberry."

The party goers were throwing confetti over Con and Anne as if they were a bride and groom. Anne was sobbing, Con laughing. Anne was passing from hug to hug like a basketball in a close game.

All that friendship.

Molly had never been a part of anything like that. Friendship rode the boat like a passenger, larger than all rest.

Confetti symbolized everything in Molly's life for which she had had high hopes . . . and then nothing came of her hopes. New Year's Eve, or Memorial Day parades — handfuls of confetti tossed high — beautiful aloft — paper rejoicing.

But for Molly the confetti was always on the pavement, to be ground underfoot by people who did not care.

Nobody hugged Molly. Gary sprang out to hug Anne like the rest, and wish her a fond farewell. Molly was left alone in the dark cabin, as the sun set and the wind strengthened.

Molly's jealousy grew, and became a thing as large and as real as the friendship she yearned for.

Jeremiah Dunstan had taken all the film he reasonably could of these kids partying. Until something interesting occurred, he didn't want to waste any more footage. How interesting would it be to look at them all milling around talking and eating?

He sat on a seat by the rail, staring back

at the wake. Smooth waves of high water spread behind them like a forked dragon's tail. A small motorized dinghy came up toward them. Jere could make out a boy at the tiller and a girl —

Look at that hair! Thick, long red hair, blowing around like a cloud, now lashing the girl's face, now tugged out behind, now caught in the boy's hand as he gestured while talking.

The dinghy pulled up close. The boy shouted, "I'm trying to deliver her to your party. She missed the boat."

Jere nodded and went to tell the captain, who nodded back, and let the engine idle so the girl could be brought aboard.

Jere found her stunning. More real than Anne, this girl was sunburnt and freckled, and laughing, her wide, happy mouth puckered in embarrassment and pleasure. That great hair didn't settle down now that the wind was gone, but stayed up, teased into a halo by the elements.

Who is this? Jere thought. I have to know!

Con and Gary helped the girl into the boat and he suddenly realized that something dramatic had happened, and he, the cameraman, had missed it entirely. He felt like asking the girl to get back in the dinghy and start over.

Her name appeared to be Beth, or Rose, or both, or maybe Rose was her last name. She was definitely popular; they were hugging her as as much as they'd hugged Anne. Or maybe this was just a hugging crowd.

Probably another graduating senior headed for parts unknown. He would ask. He would definitely ask.

Chapter 13

If Beth had had a choice, she would have
drifted all night in the dark with Blaze. She
would have moved to Arizona with him, gone
to the Arctic with him, pioneered on the moon
with him. However, it seemed premature to
announce this to Blaze, as boys were apt to
vanish at the first syllable of serious intent.

Blaze was telling her about how this had
been the longest summer of his entire life.
The family situation certainly seemed com-
plex. His mother's corporation had promoted her to a position in California; his
father's corporation had promoted him to a
position in Dallas. While his parents tried
to figure out what they were going to do,
Blaze got accepted at a college in New York
City, and his uncle and aunt in Westerly
offered to take him for the summer while his
parents moved, wherever they ended up
going. In the end, each parent had taken each

promotion and now Blaze had no real home at all.

Beth could not imagine going off in the world without having an actual place to go back *to*. She would always have Westerly, and in some way, it would always have her.

"Going to college in New York City?" she repeated. She would have to introduce him to Kip. Kip would love it. A handsome boy from Arizona to escort her her first week in town.

But would I love that? Beth asked herself. My daydream come true. Finally, around the corner, there he is, the perfect boy. So I take him on board the *Duet* and who does he have his duet with? Kip, of course. A better, brighter choice than me, anyhow. Who won't be hundreds of miles away, but right there, in the same town. Maybe even the same dorm.

Beth's heart sank. Probably in the same classes, too, she thought, majoring in the same subject. . . .

"So what will you be doing?" he asked. They all asked that. Tiredly she told him about the community college and waitressing. All her thoughtful genes won out, and Beth said, "I'll have to introduce you to a girl on board, one of my best friends, who's going to be in New York for college, too." Beth steeled herself. "You'll love her," she added. Beth tried to remember Kip's real name, since Kip intended a fresh, nickname-less start to college. "Katharine Elliott is her name," she finished, feeling saintly.

"Hey, that'd be great. I'd love that. There's only one problem, Beth. You can climb aboard, but I have to return this boat to the boat rental. Calvin didn't seem like the type to laugh if one of his boats never returned."

"Oh, if that isn't just like life!" she said crossly. "Always boats to be returned to boat rental. I hate details. Life should be free of niggly little details. You should just be able to sail on to the next happy event without worrying about boats getting returned."

He was grinning at her, and the thin features seemed momentarily hers, as if she owned them, or had blended with them. They talked about life's annoyances for a moment. "What are you going to study in college?" he asked abruptly.

He thought I was interesting, Beth Rose mused. He liked what I said about boat returns. But now I'll tell him what I'm studying and he'll laugh *at* me, not with me. If only she could answer something thrilling like astronomy or automobile design. "I kind of want to teach sixth grade," she said, "so I guess I'll study a little bit of everything."

"I loved sixth," Blaze told her. "All the good stuff is in sixth. Ancient history and Stonehenge. I remember when we got to Egypt we built pyramids out of sugar cubes. We were bringing shoe boxes to school so we could make dioramas about early agriculture."

Beth was delighted. "I loved all that," she confessed. "It was the last time I was really terrific in school. My shoe boxes were always the best."

"Not mine," Blaze said. "I'm pretty good at grades, but I haven't hit anything I want to do for a lifetime. I'm hoping to find the shoe box of my dreams at college." He stood up, started the engine on the first rip of the cord, and set a course for the *Duet*. Beth no longer felt like shouting a conversation. Why had he broken off their talk like that? Of course, it was probably just that he was fulfilling his promise to get her to the *Duet*. But maybe she had gotten boring, and he was lying about sixth grade pyramids and couldn't wait to get rid of her.

"Here we are, Beth. Throw that guy the line right behind you, okay?"

She grabbed the rope he was pointing to. It was odd, throwing a rope (which partially stayed with you) instead of a ball (which left completely). It was caught by, of all people, Con Winter, who whipped it efficiently around a cleat. The *Duet* idled, its engines quieter, and the little skiff banged gently against the tubby sides of the bigger boat.

"Hi, Con," Beth said. "The ice cream has melted away. If you wanted it solid, you should have waited for me."

Con just laughed. "The *Duet* waits for nobody," he informed her. "Sailing times are never flexible. Those who are tardy make separate voyages. Welcome aboard." He reached a hand down for her. Beth was frightened. The skiff felt awfully tippy. There didn't seem to be anywhere to step, or anything to grip with her other hand.

Gary materialized next to Con with two more hands out, and with a push from Blaze she was up and over. The boys enjoyed it, but Beth had never felt so awkward nor so heavy.

"Con?" she said. "Can Blaze come to the party, too?"

"Sure, the more the merrier. Let me ask the captain if we can just tie his boat and let it follow us in the wake."

Con darted off. Blaze, surprised and pleased, waited. Gary whispered in her ear, "So who's this, Beth?"

"This is my friend, Blaze," she said, making introductions. "Gary — Blaze."

The dark, sleek boy on board half-saluted the tanned, sharp-edged boy sitting in the bobbing skiff. It seemed to Beth they were eyeing each other very warily. Perhaps they're both in love with me, she thought, and they're checking out the competition.

She laughed to herself. It was just dark, and they had to narrow their eyes to see each other.

"Captain says no problem," Con informed

them. "He saw the skiff; he's going to radio Calvin Rentals to tell him this one'll be in later."

They retied the skiff in another location and yanked Blaze aboard. Con said that any friend of Beth's was a friend of his, which was certainly news to Beth. Beth began introducing Blaze to everybody. It was enormous fun. Blaze was good-looking, and completely unknown. Where Beth could have found a boyfriend from Arizona in the few hours since they had seen her last was something they were dying to know. In honor of the occasion, Blaze put his shirt back on and accepted a Coke.

"Blaze, this is my friend Anne," began Beth Rose, "the party's for her. And this is my friend Susan. And my friend Mike. And my — "

Molly? What was she doing here? They had not invited her! They would never invite her! It was unthinkable to have Molly — who had tried to get Con to abandon Anne when she was pregnant — who had tried to get Anne falsely arrested only last New Year's Eve —

Beth wanted to throw her right overboard.

But there she stood, smiling at Blaze, her little head with its cute new haircut turned to the side, so that her earrings danced. Elfin. Adorable.

She's a troll, Beth Rose thought grimly, waiting under a bridge to capture the innocent.

But Beth had introduced everybody else as "my friend so and so." She couldn't change the pattern, it would be too cruel, too obvious. She didn't want Blaze to think she could be mean to people she didn't like.

"And this is my friend Molly," said Beth unwillingly.

Chapter 14

Matthew O'Connor felt as if he had lost both sight and hearing. Maybe muscle coordination as well. Around him a party whirled — there was shouting, dancing, laughing, talking. He felt like somebody who had spent too long on a carnival ride, and got off with a distorted sense of balance, and was staggering across the grass, trying to get hold of his own brain.

The music was like a headache, punching him.

He could not bring himself to look in Emily's direction. She was standing all hunched over, as if she expected to be struck by something — or had been already. But *she*'s the one who struck *me*! Matt thought. Throwing away my ring?

Everywhere he turned, his eyes seemed to land on diamonds — stars in the sky, sparkles in the water, gleams off ice in glasses, glitters from other girls' earrings.

Matt had loved choosing that ring, selling his car to pay for it; he had loved the tiny velvet box it came in and the feel of Emily's hand when he slid it on. He had felt powerful, like a rescuer. Now he felt limp, like a failure.

Emily had had a difficult childhood. Her parents weren't very nice people, and it was hard to find anything good to say about either one. He used to marvel at how sweet, generous Emily could have sprung from two mean, thoughtless manipulators like the Edmundsons. When the parents decided on a divorce, they virtually abandoned Emily in the process. Emily had ended up living with Anne for quite a while, and Matt had wanted her to stay with his own family, a suggestion his mother squashed in a hurry.

Through it all she remained sweet and funny and amiable. Matt had thought that nothing could shake Emily; that she could go through hell smiling.

So now he had a great job, would be away for a few months, and she was acting as if their lives together were over.

Thrown away his ring! Why didn't she just give it back to me? he thought.

He imagined a date in which his girl handed him back his ring. I would have thrown it away myself, he realized. Or thrown it at her.

Emily pointed suddenly, her hand white in the dark. "There's Con. With Gary and Mike and those new boys. You wanted to tell the guys all about your fabulous job, Matt. Here's your chance. Con is dying for a change of subject, he's sick of hearing about Anne's terrific job, so tell him about *your* terrific job instead. Let them all be jealous of *you* for a while."

He shrank from the bitterness in her voice.

How much of my proposal of marriage was because I wanted to be the Good Guy who rescues the Girl? And now she's better; she's living with her father; she's come to terms with both her parents and she doesn't need rescuing. The pressure's off. I can go do my own thing instead.

But Emily had never put pressure on him. If anything, she was the one who had been reluctant to get engaged to start with. *He* had pressured *her*.

Confused thoughts rose and collapsed in his head like patterns in a kaleidoscope.

He knew he was wrong and yet he knew he was right.

"Emily," he said thickly, "we have to talk."

Her pixie face was white and pinched in the shadows. "You mean you have to talk me into seeing things your way," she said. She walked away from him.

He didn't follow her. If they couldn't talk alone, they certainly couldn't talk in front of all these people. Matt, who loved crowds and parties, felt swamped in voices and personalities. There were too many people; he could not distinguish them, he could not even care about them. All he wanted was for this not to be happening.

Emily slipped into the press of kids. How involved with their own lives they were! They had their own problems and jobs and families and loves and hates — they neither knew nor cared about Emily's. Nobody would notice that she and Matt were silent in the dark. Nobody would peer down at her left hand to see that her ring was gone. It was nobody's responsibility to see that she had a good time at Anne's party, and nobody would notice if she didn't.

If I want to talk this out, she thought, I have to grab a friend, haul her away, hand her the facts on a platter.

But the only person she could really talk to was Matt himself.

Why am I being so horrible to him? she thought. I rejoice for Anne going abroad. I rejoice for Kip getting in the school she worked so hard for. Why can't I rejoice for Matt, because all his skills took him in the direction he's best at?

Matt's perfectly right, it isn't the end of the world; we can still be engaged, we can still get married someday.

She walked up to the counters. The real food had not yet been brought out. There was still the chips, dips, vegetable sticks, crackers, cheese, and peanuts. Emily felt if she did not have solid food pretty soon she would faint. She took another soda. She had had so much carbonated junk tonight she was one big bubble.

It's because I am the one left behind, she thought. The person going has a destination. The person left just sits and mopes. There is nothing worse than being the one left behind.

She heaved a huge, painful sigh.

She would have to go over to Anne's house tomorrow, after Anne had left for the airport. She would have to say to Mrs. Stephens, "Hi, my diamond ring is in your grass. I brought my brush and comb, do you mind if I comb your whole yard looking for it?"

Chapter 15

Not one girl on board the *Duet* had ever enjoyed what Beth Rose Chapman was enjoying at that moment. Not even Anne, unarguably the most lovely girl who ever went to Westerly High. Not even Molly, who had gone out with an awful lot of boys. Not Kip, nor Emily, nor Susan, nor Lynda.

For Beth Rose was surrounded by three boys.

Gary, whom she had dated a year before, was definitely back and definitely interested.

Blaze, whom she had picked up on the dock just that afternoon, was also present and interested.

And Jere, whom they had written off as some employee carrying a camera, was inching forward, getting closer.

And Beth, like any girl flirting with three boys who flirted with her first, was having the time of her life. The girls were angry and hurt. It was not fair that they should have none and Beth Rose three. They almost forgot their envy of Anne, as they stared at Beth.

Beth was sitting on a bench, her knees crossed, and the soft cloth of her yellow dress flowing around her. On her right sat Gary, whom she was facing, and into whose eyes she laughed. Above her perched Blaze, sitting on the brass rail, elbow on knees and face in hands, so he was hunched right down between Beth and Gary. And sitting cross-legged at her left, sprawled on the glossy deck, was Jere.

"It's like she's holding court," said one girl.

"Somebody go bother them with potato chips and celery sticks," said another girl.

"Somebody tell that band to start playing," said a more intelligent one. "She can only dance with one at a time."

"Good idea. And we'll get to see which one she cares about most, too. That's the one she'll dance with."

The others knew better. Beth Rose wouldn't do the asking. The boy who danced with her would simply be the one who asked first. Lynda suggesting placing bets but nobody would bet; it made them too irritable. Right at that moment, no matter how wonderful her own future looked, there was not a girl on the deck who would not have exchanged places with Beth Rose.

The combo — two guitars and a drummer

—set up on the open upper deck and began playing the current number three on the charts. The party abandoned the chips and dip, and the soda and peanuts, and swarmed up the narrow, almost vertical, metal stairs to dance in the moonlight.

Anne and Con were already there, dancing the first dance.

Molly was not shy. She had nothing to lose, and no worries, and hadn't Beth Rose introduced her as a friend? *She* was not going to that upper deck without a partner in tow. Molly walked right up to the quartet of Gary, Blaze, Jere, and Beth Rose. She perched on the railing next to Blaze. "Hi there, everybody." She reserved her smile for Blaze.

He smiled back. "Hello, Molly."

She was immensely pleased. He had remembered her name. "Blaze, I don't want you to feel like a stranger. How about a dance?"

He looked startled more than anything else, but he hopped off the railing with her and off they went.

Beth Rose watched them go. Of course, Blaze could hardly have retorted that he liked feeling strange and would Molly please buzz off. Still, she would have liked. . . .

Con Winter leaned over the upper deck railing and yelled down to her group. "Hey! Jeremiah Dunstan! What do you think you were hired for? Get up here and film the dancing. You already missed Anne and me alone for the first dance. Now when you film it, it'll be fake."

The boy Jere, whom Beth had scarcely met, got silently up from the deck, picked up his camera and vanished.

Well! thought Beth. Didn't take long for my circle of admirers to dwindle. She was very aware of Gary's presence. After a long absence he was next to her again. Of course with Gary it was hard to tell if this meant a thing. She hoped he would ask her to dance; he was a wonderful dancer. But he didn't. He talked to her about the restaurant, and how his father had agreed Gary could help design the addition, and how hard it was to hire and keep busboys.

How could Gary, who had once seemed perfect to her, be boring? Beth changed the subject rather than think less of Gary. "Doesn't the idea of all our group going on to other things make you feel like a part of history?" she said to him. "We're even in a book. Caught there, in our yearbook, in black and white, like a text. We are the past."

Gary blinked. He said maybe he would drink another soda. She said she'd have one, too. "Do you look at your yearbook much?" she asked him when they reached the bar.

"I've never looked at it once. It ended with high school."

Beth kept her yearbook propped open. Into the page where Emily's photograph smiled out at her, Beth had slid Emily's engagement announcement. On Anne's page went the newspaper's early May interview of Ivory Glynn and the brief announcement from the PEOPLE page about Anne's job. From the high school guidance department column, she had snipped many a one-liner ". . . and we are proud that our brilliant Katharine Elliott has been accepted at no less than four top schools. . . ."

"You'll be the class historian then," Gary said. "You're going to be the only one left anyway, so you can read the papers and keep up with it all. Hey, look, real food! What are those?" he asked the waiter.

Four vast, deep, hot trays were being laid out. "Lasagna, eggplant parmigiana, ravioli, and cheese manicotti."

"I'm in heaven now," Gary said. "Who would want to dance when there's decent food around?"

Beth laughed. "Normally I would argue the point, but so far today I have had one banana and one yogurt. Pass the plates, I'll be the first into the lasagna."

He isn't interested, Beth thought. She slid the large serving spoon into the casserole, and steam rose from the cut in the noodles. I'm not going to be the only one left in Westerly; he'll be here, too. But he didn't mention that. I don't think he thinks of it that way. High school is so far behind Gary he doesn't even feel part of it. Whereas with me it was half an hour ago, it could start again in the morning. I wouldn't be at all surprised if somebody asked me what the English assignment was.

"Careful," Gary said, "you don't want tomato sauce all over that yellow dress."

"It'll blend right in with the ice cream," said Beth. "Did you know I missed the boat and melted the ice cream?"

"I knew you missed the boat, but I figured the sun melted the ice cream."

Beth fell back in love with Gary again. Honestly, other girls seemed to have such solid reasons for loving a guy. All a boy had to do to win Beth was make a feeble joke and she was his. She kissed Gary suddenly and he looked up, surprised.

Con was a more vigorous dancer than Anne, who liked to be graceful in all things and didn't get wild and crazy for hard rock numbers. But she would rather dance than talk tonight, considering the various pitfalls between herself and Con, so she danced.

After the fourth number there was a momentary musical pause. Susan and Lynda cornered them. "Anne, I'm *dying* for details," moaned Susan. "I think all the time about what you'll be doing, you lucky, lucky thing. Tell me *exactly* what happens, beginning with the morning."

"Is it true that Ivory Glynn is going to be

on David Letterman the first night you're in New York?" asked Lynda.

"When I was in New York City, we couldn't afford to stay in any of the spectacular hotels, like the Waldorf, but we walked into the lobbies. Will you be staying in places like that?"

Con stiffened. They wouldn't bother to ask what *he* was doing. He was just another college freshman, indistinguishable from any other, taking freshman English, and going out for football, and probably not making it, what with the competition he faced.

Whereas Anne had gotten the job in a million without any effort at all. Con's cheek muscles twitched.

Anne said, "Of course I won't be on the show, but she will be a guest of David's and I *will* be backstage with Miss Glynn, so who knows — I could meet almost anybody back there!"

Susan and Lynda sighed in happy envy.

Anne talked on and on. She might actually have been on a stage, with a spotlight. She already had fans, that was for sure. They did not tire of her stories and they did not rejoin the dancing.

Con shouted, "Dinner is served below!"

It was very late for most of them to be starting supper. There was a general stampede for the food. "Let's go, Anne," Con said sharply.

"We'll be there in a minute," Susan said,

without looking back at him, and Anne kept right on talking and did not look at Con, either.

Talking about herself, Con thought, always about herself, never about me.

His cheek twitched painfully.

Kip had chosen cheese manicotti, and piled on salad and two rolls, and was balancing this while talking to Mike. She had cornered him carefully. She was not entirely sure what her own motives were. They couldn't date again; too far apart, and she didn't want Mike anyhow, she wanted somebody better. But she wanted to be friends again, or have Mike admit he would miss her, or at least get a real smile from him before they parted ways.

But it was as awkward as it had been since the day they split up. "Oh, come on," she said, suddenly irritated. "We were so close for a while, don't you want to — ?"

"No."

"I'm not asking for a date, Mike. I'll be hundreds of miles away till next June. I just want us to be —"

"You have to keep bringing up where *you're* going to school, huh, Kip? Just because some of us didn't get accepted where we wanted, and ended up going to State with jocks like Con who can hardly even read."

Kip choked on her manicotti. Con was standing right next to them. Con sucked in his breath. "Hi, Mike," he said deliberately.

Mike's lasagna fell off his fork. "Hey, Con. Just joking."

"Uh-huh." Con waved his plate of ravioli and one of the little squares flew off and made a tomato-plopping sound against the deck. "Kip bothering you, Mikey? Be a man, you can talk back."

"Oh, the way you've figured out how to talk back to Anne?" Mike said.

Kip tried to be a peacemaker. "I'm trying to be friends with Mike again, Con, and he won't cooperate. I don't think I'm good enough for him."

Con laughed. "You don't think that at all, Kip. You figure *we're* not good enough for *you*. *You* have to go all the way to New York City to find anybody worthy of *your* special talents."

Kip lost her temper. "Yeah, well, *Anne* decided she'd have to cross the *ocean* to find anybody worthy, Con Winter."

All the guests were eating quietly, listening to this argument as it boiled. Molly listened hardest. This will be fun, she thought. We'll have a food fight. I've never had a really, truly food fight. And with Italian food, too. Now *that* will be a send-off for Anne!

Chapter 16

Con Winter was in a fighting mood. He couldn't fight Anne. There was no football team here so he could legitimately fight quarterbacks and tight ends. He was ready to fight anybody at all.

He looked around, eyes passing Kip, which angered her, because she considered herself a worthy opponent for Con any day of the week. He skipped Gary, who was too amiable for fights, and Mike who wasn't interested in his problems. His eyes landed on the new boy — Blaze.

Who was this Blaze, anyway? he thought. Somebody Beth dragged on board. "What kind of a name is Blaze?" demanded Con. "Sounds like something for a horse. A name a nine-year-old would pick out if he had a stable and a paddock."

There was an astonished silence, while all the listeners tried to figure out what Blaze had done to bring that on, and while Blaze got to his feet and wondered what was going to happen next.

Molly was in the mood to keep the sparks flying. She slithered between the two angry boys and smiled up into Con's face. "You have a rather interesting name, too, darling. Con, as in con artist."

Con glared at her. "You're the con artist, Molly. You have to be or you wouldn't be on board. For sure nobody invited you. Who'd you con this time?"

Slowly, several feet off, Jeremiah Dunstan shouldered his camcorder again and inched up on the stairs for a better perspective. He needed more light, but putting on the hot beam from the camera would alert the subjects, so he filmed it in the shadows.

"Anne asked me," Molly said.

"She did not," Con said.

"Did so. Hey, Emily, wasn't I over at Anne's with you this afternoon?"

Emily had hardly been listening. She was gripping her bare left hand as if she thought she could make the ring materialize. "Yes, you were," she said woodenly.

Molly laughed. "See, Con?" She stood before him, her legs spread for balance against the slight rocking of the boat. He held his plate of ravioli, and Molly held her soda. They might have been weapons for a duel, the way the two of them paused in hostility.

Jeremiah leaned far forward to get a better profile of Con in a rage. It was nice to know that Con actually had another expression other than Mr. Perfect Body with the Blow-Dry Hair.

But Con caught the movement. "We have another stupid name over here," he said, pointing. "Jere. Rhymes with hair. What's it stand for, little Jere?"

The boy lowered his camera. "Jeremiah."

"Kind of a fat old name," Con observed. "Beards and robes go with it. You're the one who should be named Blaze. Blaze is a good name for somebody who actually thinks he can go straight from making stupid little backyard home movies to California and box office hits."

Jere tried to remind himself the customer was always right. He tried to tell himself he liked earning money this way. He tried to tell himself he should make allowances for jerks like Con Winter.

Kip began wondering just what Con had in his glass. Would ginger ale have that effect? Was he really so jealous of Anne for taking off like a rocket that he had to attack his guests? Kip was glad Anne was still up on the top deck cornered by her fans. With any luck, poor Anne would never see this scene. Kip would smooth it over for her sake. "Now, now," Kip said, "why don't we all cool down? Here, Con, how about some more ginger ale?"

"You know what you can do with your ginger ale?" demanded Con. "It's bad enough you bossed the whole high school for four years; don't try to boss me at my own party."

"Somebody should throw you in the river," said Kip contemptuously. "That would cool you off."

"Somebody should throw *you* in," Con retorted. "You couldn't boss the whole show from there."

Kip's temper was worse than Con's any day. She lost it totally, and it was Kip who hurled the first food. Her glass of ginger ale went right in Con's face and her half-full plate all over his shirt.

Jere lifted his camera again. A real food fight — what footage it would be! — worth all the insults!

The party guests stood frozen for a moment, as Con retaliated with his own ravioli. But Kip was not an athlete for nothing. She leaped out of the way, and the ravioli splattered red and tomato-y all over Blaze.

There was a horrified silence.

The food fight stopped before it began.

The new boy? The boy who had never met anybody in Westerly but them? The one Con had just insulted over his name? *He* was the one covered with food?

Several couples melted away. They didn't want any part of it. They slid past Jere and his camera and filled the upper deck, dancing as if they had never left.

Blaze wiped tomato from his eyes and hair. "I was complaining that this was the most boring summer of my life. Guess I have to shelve that complaint. I am no longer bored. A little grubby, but right in the action."

Even Con had to be impressed by that reaction. Con sagged a little and muttered half an apology. Kip was horrified by what she had done to both of them and, as always, did things to excess, apologizing left and right. "Okay, okay," said Con wearily, "forget it, Kip. Just — "

But he stared down at himself, an absolute mess, and did not know what she or he should do next.

Molly walked right up and slid her arm through Blaze's wet one. "Blaze, what kind of swimmer are you?"

"The best," he told her.

"I'm pretty fair myself," said Molly, grinning. "And the best place to get cleaned off is right there below us." She pointed to the river.

Blaze laughed. He and Molly climbed up on the railing and jumped right into the water.

Beth Rose Chapman could not believe this. It would have been crummy but altogether reasonable to lose wonderful Blaze to wonderful Kip. But to lose Blaze to rotten Molly?

Molly and Blaze splashed and laughed and swam alongside the *Duet*. They were having more fun than anybody, which seemed the height of unfairness. Beth sat disconsolately on the step next to the boy with the movie camera. "You run with a strange crowd," he observed.

"They run," said Beth glumly. "I just sit."

Jere laughed. "Do you also dance? And if so, may I join you?"

The *Duet* chugged along. She was a tubby old thing, more a ferry than a speedboat. The black river was glossy in the moonlight and punctuated by laughter and splashing it seemed a lovely place to be. Kip was envious of Blaze and Molly.

Con wasn't. "I hope they drown," he said.

"Oh, Con, you do not."

"Kip, for once in your life could you stop giving people orders? I know what I hope and you don't."

His voice was tired, and it hurt Kip far more than if he had been yelling at her.

She knew she liked to take charge, but she didn't like to think of herself as bossy. What if I really don't have a very nice personality? she thought. What if I get to college and nobody likes me? What if I really do have to come back here a failure?

"I feel like swimming, too," Kip said.

They had both been swim team captains. Con's team had come in second in regional competitions, Kip's had not placed. The two teams, `men and women, had not swum against each other. Kip had wanted to be first regionally just to swagger in front of the boys at the high school. Now she was ashamed of herself.

"Hey, pull us up, will you?" Blaze said.

Kip and Con were the only ones left by the rail. Everybody else was sitting down to eat, or back upstairs dancing. They pulled Blaze up first, and then Molly.

"Con, you still have ravioli all over you," said Kip. "I'm really sorry. If you take off your shirt I'll try to clean it off for you."

He shrugged and left his shirt on.

He thought of his choices for the evening. He could rejoin Anne. Which would make him mad again. Refill his plate. He wasn't hungry anymore. Find Gary and Mike. They'd laugh at him for the food fight with Kip.

He said, "Hey, Kippie, you always wanted to see if the women's team could beat the men's. I'll race you. Let's see who can dive off the boat, swim to Swallow Island, and get back to the boat first."

Chapter 17

Blaze was enjoying Molly. She was a very funny person. The way she was willing to drip-dry in the evening breeze appealed to Blaze. None of this rushing off to find a blow-dryer for her hair, or scurrying to a mirror to check her mascara. Blaze hated girls who were preoccupied with their faces.

Blaze and Molly fixed themselves huge dishes of food and retreated to a dark corner. Two more nice things. She wasn't going to claim she was on a diet, never touched fattening stuff, or had to worry about an extra ounce. And — this boat was full of dark corners.

He was sorry to find that Molly would be staying in Westerly and it was that bossy girl Kip who would be in college in New York at the same time he was. "Wish it could be the other way around," he said to Molly.

Molly just smiled. She was fairly cynical about compliments from boys. But she was a good listener, and sat through long stories about his life in Arizona, his parental job-split situation, and his boring summer here in Westerly.

"Westerly is kind of the back of the world," she agreed. She saw her own life, forever set in Westerly, never moving on. She shivered.

"So how come you're not headed out, like every other Super Power on this boat?" Blaze asked.

Molly giggled. She liked him calling Anne and Kip and their sort Super Powers. "I just didn't plan," she admitted. " I didn't know it would be like this — over and done with. I guess I thought I'd go to high school forever."

He asked her quite a bit about Westerly High and her friends there. She didn't give him much in the way of answers. What could she say — that she had crashed to get on board? That nobody here qualified as a friend of Molly Nelmes? That Beth had lied introducing her that way?

Molly had wanted a lot of things from boys over the years: affection, attention, fast cars, money spent, good times, a companion for hanging out. But for this thin, dark boy with his sharp, thin features, his eyes that drilled into hers and his soft laugh, she felt something different. She wanted his good opinion.

I want him to think I'm terrific, she realized. I want him to think I'm nice. But I'm not either one.

Molly ate less, and swallowed with difficulty.

"That was really nice of you," said Blaze suddenly, "jumping into the fray there when Con was giving me a hard time about my name."

Molly had to set down her fork so it wouldn't tremble. Had anybody ever thanked her for doing something nice? Had she ever *done* anything nice to get thanked *for*? "Con is a jerk," she said briefly.

"But who is he?" Blaze asked. "Who are any of these kids?"

Her opinions were low. Con was a shallow Big Man on Campus, who, like his girlfriend Anne, had achieved everything just by standing there and being pretty. Beth was a nonentity with great hair. Kip was a show-off who tried to run the world. Emily was —

Emily.

Molly touched the ring on her finger.

Crazy, that's what Emily was.

Molly took a breath to tell Blaze exactly what she thought of every guest on board the *Duet*, but something stopped her. If I say ugly things, she thought, he won't think I'm nice. Molly struggled to think of nice things, therefore, but nothing came to mind. Finally she said, "Con's always gotten his way. From swim team to Anne. Now he's not getting his way. It's a kid's tantrum, that's all."

Blaze accepted this. He set his plate down on the bench next to hers. "Finished?"

"Stuffed."

"Want to dance?"

They danced right where they were, away from the others, cramped by boat equipment. "This party," said Blaze after a while, "has worn me out."

"I can imagine. How many parties involve food fights, insults, and swimming to clean off your clothes?"

Blaze laughed. "Listen," he said uncomfortably, "you're the second really nice person I've met. Beth Rose is the other one. I know this sounds dumb, but I'll only be in Westerly a few more days. I hate to waste them. You and Beth are such good friends. Do you think maybe both of you would sort of — oh — run around with me and do stuff next week? Just as — you know — friends?"

Surely, thought Beth Rose, the strangest sight I have ever seen is Kip holding hands with Con, leaping over the side, and swimming toward Swallow Island in the night.

Who could imagine Kip and Con doing anything together ever? Who would want to do anything as horrid as swim in the dark anyhow? What if your foot touched something? Ick. It could be anything from a fish that bit, to a dead body.

If the captain of the *Duet* knew, he would surely refuse permission. It had to be dangerous. Of course, by day they all swam in the

Westerly River, and the best swimming was off Swallow Island. Still. . . .

She listened to splashing. Jere put his camera back down. Too dark now to take films. Beth could no longer tell if the water noises were Kip and Con swimming, or somebody far away on a dock kicking his bare feet in the water, or killer sharks. She giggled.

"What?" said Jere.

"I decided I don't have to worry if killer sharks are going to eat them."

"Very few killer sharks in Westerly River," agreed Jere, laughing. "Want something more to eat? We have to keep a vigil here and be keepers of the finish line. Those two strike me as very competitive types who will not want their judges to be off dancing when they get back."

"You don't think anything could happen to them, do you?" Beth said.

Jere considered it. Beth Rose liked how he didn't just laugh off her worry, but gave it real thought. Not like her parents, or Gary, or even Anne, all of whom would sometimes study the ceiling when she worried about something and moan, "Oh, Beth, *really*." Jere said, "This is a pretty tame river. I've spent my life on it or in it. Hard to imagine what could happen except they could get tired. Both captains of swim teams . . . I'm not going to call the water police about them, if that's what you mean."

Beth filled her plate mostly with salad. This was not for diet reasons, but because she had already had helpings of manicotti and eggplant and half a loaf of Italian bread slathered with butter. "You," she accused Jere, "had the garlic bread."

"I know. I'm sorry. I love the stuff. Here. I'll hide behind my camera."

"No. I'll have garlic bread, too. Then we'll have matching garlic breath."

They ate quietly, savoring flavor and texture. Little flakes of bread crust fell on their clothes. Beth wanted to brush them off Jere, but stopped herself. She was not quite ready for the return gesture. Now and then Jere touched his camera the way a girl touches her purse, to reassure himself it was there and safe by his feet. "Don't film me eating," Beth said. "Or doing anything else. I don't want to be immortalized."

"You're the only one. Most people love it." He told her about his jobs — bar mitzvahs and family reunions, church picnics and school graduations. She was fascinated, and asked great questions, each one letting him tell more and more details about himself. Jere loved to talk about himself. With an effort, he remembered that it was only fair to let Beth talk about herself, too. "So what are you going to do now that you've graduated?"

"I've had to answer that question ten hundred times," wailed Beth. "Nine hundred of them tonight."

"Sorry. Forget it. Keep the future to your-self. Have more garlic bread, then nobody else will ask you anything tonight."

She laughed. Jere was getting a real thing for her hair. It seemed unaffected by gravity. When she shook her head, her crazy red hair flew around and stayed up. He wondered how Beth would react to a very garlicky kiss. He took a light breath, and thought about it in detail.

Beth Rose was contemplating the last two pieces of the garlic loaf. "Other kids are deciding whether to go to Rome or Paris," he teased her. "You're trying to decide whether to have another slice of bread." He kissed her cheek very lightly. It made him so nervous he was completely exhausted by it, but it was so pleasurable he was filled with enough energy to do it all night.

"Beth?" he said, passing her the garlic bread, "what are you doing tomorrow?"

Molly Nelmes didn't know whether to laugh or to cry. She and Beth Rose were sup-posed to escort Blaze for the rest of the summer? She could just imagine walking up to Beth with that request. "Hey, Beth, old friend? I know you hate and despise me, for good reason, of course, and I know I find you about as interesting as mismatched socks in a dark laundry room, but let's show Blaze the world of Westerly, huh? Sound like fun? Think we can pull it off?"

She said, "I'd love to run around with you for a few days, Blaze. I don't know what Beth's plans are, though."

He teased her about her days-Blaze rhyme.

Molly thought, How can he possibly like me at the same time he likes Beth Rose? And what happens if Beth Rose and I like him at the same time?

"Let's join the others on the upper deck," she said. "I should introduce you to more of them."

"I don't think I want to meet more of them," said Blaze. "They're Con's friends, right? So who needs them?"

Molly was crazy about him. About his name and his tan, and his thin nose, which she wanted to trace with the tip of her finger. She had never wanted to touch anybody so much.

And how wonderful — what icing on a perfect cake — to have him more interested in her than in any friends of Con Winter!

Molly put forth her hand, to drag him up, but he took the hand and did not budge. In a very strange voice Blaze said, "You're wearing an engagement ring."

Chapter 18

Matt O'Connor tried to think about his job. Racing cars. The wonderful hot smell of tires leaving patches on asphalt. The feel of the tools and the frenzy of speed. And so much would be at stake! He would be on probation and if he didn't fit in, wasn't good enough, couldn't get along with the crew, then he'd be out.

It was a life that made Matt hot with excitement. Or had. Now it sounded like a paragraph he was reading in *Popular Science* or *Sports Illustrated*. Something other men did. Something far removed from his real existence.

Matt watched Kip and Con swim away. He was envious. He'd love to swim away from this problem. And he wouldn't swim back, either.

The important thing, he told himself, is to stay nonviolent.

He was grateful for the noise ordinance

that meant they'd have to get off the river shortly. No power boats past ten-thirty. Con had had to get a special permit to have the fireworks. Although no doubt Kip had actually done that for him, too.

Matt glimpsed Emily. She was alone. Holding a plate she had not touched. Probably wasn't going to touch, since she had picked up no fork. She looked very small.

On the other side of the cabin, Matt could hear girls talking. "There's enough food down there to sink the *Duet*," said one.

"One duet aboard this ship already sank," giggled another girl. "Matt and Emily are over. Done. Split. She isn't wearing her ring anymore."

"Yeah?" said the first, with intense interest. "What happened? You know any details?"

"No. Let's corner Emily and get them."

The gossiping girls laughed almost wildly.

Matt felt ill. Em would hate having to tell people she wasn't friends with what had happened. He moved quickly to get to Em first. "Stick with me," he said to her without preliminaries, "there are some Class A gossips en route to talk to you." He took her plate, shoveled more food on it, grabbed forks and napkins, and retreated with Emily to the stuffy little cabin.

"We can't talk here," murmured Emily, waving at a group of friends who had most of the seats already.

"You don't want to talk anyhow, do you?" Matt said.

She shrugged infinitesimally. Which probably meant Yes, she did want to talk. Matt balanced the plate and moved on with her, trying to find privacy. Finally they sat on a bench — but not close. There was room for another couple between them. In fact, conversation was so awkward, it felt like there had to be another two or three people there — invisible but interfering.

Matt heard faint splashing. Was it Kip or Con coming in first? It would matter so much to each of them, and it would not matter to anybody else at all. What matters to me? thought Matthew O'Connor. Do I even know? He said, "Emily, okay. I won't go." The words wrenched him, like the bolt on a wheel. Metal scraped metal. I want to go, I want to go, his heart said. "I wanted to have my cake and eat it, too," he said, quoting his mother and Marie Antoinette. "I guess that was pretty adolescent." But *I'm* adolescent! he thought. And I want to go.

Matt tried to crush down the vision of the race cars. He felt as if he were crushing himself as well.

Emily just sat there. She kept a watch on the food on Matt's plate, as if it had some special significance never previously noted; as if she could read fortunes in the leftover tomato sauce, the way old ladies of yore had read fortunes in tea leaves.

She felt like a glass Christmas ornament, trod underfoot, nothing left but tiny, dangerous glass splinters. If she told Matt that announcement made her happy, it would be a lie. She did not want to be his sacrifice. She wanted to be his first choice. But if she told Matt to take the job, she would still be unhappy. Still be left behind.

Emily could think of nothing to say.

She took Matt's hand and held it tightly. When she had to wipe tears off her cheeks, she used his hand as well as hers, and finally she moved next to him, and they put their arms around each other. But it was only comfort, and not love.

Now how are you supposed to answer a question like that? thought Beth Rose. I hate that kind of question. It is unfair and bad manners.

If I say I'm not doing anything, and smile at him, I make it clear I'm expecting him to ask me out. And maybe all he was doing was asking what interesting things I might be up to on the last Sunday in August. And maybe he'll tell me what interesting things he's up to on the last Sunday in August.

If I say I'm busy, though, he might think it's a brush off, and he won't ask me out even though he was planning to. If I lie, and say I'm not busy, when I really am busy, and after that lie, he —

Her mind spilled over the possibilities for answers and misunderstandings, flirtations and irritations. She fell in love with him and out of love with him. She saw a handsome young man with a mischievous grin who had just given her a garlic-laden kiss, and she saw a dumb kid a year younger who kept fondling the camera by his sneakers.

"My big plan for the day involves my radio, the beach, and a hot dog with chili and onions from the concession," said Beth. "Want to come? Or do you have something else in mind?" There. That was making it pretty darn clear.

"Oh. Well, would you rather go to a wedding? I'm filming one over in Raulston. They let you eat all you want at the reception, and we could dance, too, if we dress right. I get bored at those things. I'm the only outsider. I have to circle around and be sure I've filmed everybody with everybody else. But it would be fun if I had company."

An invitation to a wedding. That was a novel date. Although he had not used the word "date." If I had company, was his phrase. Beth Rose wondered for the millionth time if boys analyzed little scraps of words at the same rate that girls did.

"*Your* company," added Jere, when she didn't answer.

Which was a phrase that, even to Beth, did not require heavy analysis.

* * *

The thing Kip Elliott loved about sports was that the goal was so definite. You knew where you were going. There was a finish line, or a basket, or a post. And you didn't labor on forever. You had a timer, or a quarter, or a ten-second limit.

All her life she had swum off Swallow Island. Now she swam with all her strength, to get away from the fears this party had aroused. She did not want to think of what could go wrong in her life. Only of what must surely go right.

She wanted to beat Con. She wanted to beat everybody.

Was it wrong to want to be a winner all the time? But who would want to be a loser? Who would wake up in the morning, crying, "Hey, great day, sun is shining, think I'll go out and be mediocre!" Of course not. Normal people wake up and cry, "Hey, think I'll take on the world!"

So why, thought Kip in grief, why do they just accuse me of being bossy? Can a person take on the world and not be bossy? Are presidents ever not bossy? Would you hire a captain of industry if he didn't like to be the boss? Would you elect a senator if he said he didn't like taking charge?

I am what I am, thought Katharine Elliott. Con may insult me all he likes, and call me bossy, but that's not what I am. I am organized to win, is what I am.

She swam with powerful strokes that

pulled her swiftly through the water. The currents in Westerly River were gentle. She knew in a moment it would be shallow, and she'd flounder a little, staggering out on the sand, yelling to Con that she had made it. Kip kicked deeper, but felt nothing. It was strange, swimming in the dark. She could hardly tell where Swallow Island was, and she could no longer hear Con.

Because I'm ahead of him, thought Kip.

No other reason was acceptable.

Anne Stephens was beginning to be painfully aware that Con had not been by her side in a long time. She detached herself from the group that had gathered around her and wandered around the *Duet*, trying to be casual. Con was not with Gary and Mike, his buddies. Not flirting with Molly. Not near Beth Rose, who herself was extremely near to that camera boy.

How amazing, Anne thought. Beth came aboard with that new boy Blaze and now she's kissing that new boy Jere. Imagine Beth Rose, on a social whirl!

Anne checked the cabin, below decks, the dance deck. No Con.

Great, she thought. He's so mad at me he jumped overboard. (Which was actually a rather flattering thought.)

The boat reached Lincoln Bridge. It swung gently in a long slow circle for the return journey to its dock. All the shadows slid in dark slithery shafts to face the other way. The boat's lights were bright but every rail, step, stair, and cabin cast pools of dark that changed and deepened.

Light washed over Beth Rose's face, and then Beth drowned in the dark, and Anne could see only a fraction of Beth's face.

A ship of ghosts, Anne thought.

"Anne, come over here!" Beth called. "Have you met Jeremiah Dunstan?"

"No. It's so nice of you to be taking films for us, Jere," she told him, as if she thought this was a friendly good-bye gesture on his part, and not a paid job.

Jere said he hoped she'd have a great time abroad, and asked about her itinerary.

It was less than twelve hours till her New York flight, but it seemed less real than ever. Anne said instead, "I was looking for Con."

"You won't believe this," Beth Rose told her, "but he and Kip are having a race to see who can swim quickest out to Swallow Island and back."

"I can't hear them," Jere said. "Probably got to the island and are out on the sand arguing about who touched land first."

Anne disliked swimming. If she had to swim, she used only pools where you could see the bottom, the sides, and everything else in the water with you. Nothing would make her swim in Westerly River — and at *night*?

"They're crazy," she said.

Nobody argued.

Chapter 19

Somehow, in the dark, they had swum apart. Perhaps it was early on, when they hit the wake of the *Duet*. Small waves, but Kip had headed slightly to the right, and Con to the left. Con was sure she was going to miss the whole island if she kept at that angle and he called to her, "Hey, where you going?"

"To win the race, dummy."

She was closer than he had thought, but still he could not see her. Con was wasting valuable time worrying about it; in a race you had to think of your own speed and destination, not somebody else's. He swam hard. He loved the pull of his own muscles. Con loved athletics. No matter how angry or irritable you were, if you ran hard, fought hard, or hit hard, you felt so much better.

With each powerful stroke he calmed down.

After a while he heard noise from Kip. Then she shouted, "I made it, I'm first, Con."

He swam harder but did not touch bottom. Kip splashed loudly as she raced back in for the return swim. He touched sand, staggered onto the beach, and resisted the temptation to cheat. Fully out of the water he yelled back, "Swim harder, Katharine Elliott! You'll never win this one!"

He raced back in. It was strangely difficult to get his bearings. The *Duet* was out of sight, probably by Lincoln Bridge where the water widened and turns were easy. But this was a dark stretch of river, and the few twinkling lights on shore told Con nothing. He swam hard, but nervously. A racer without a goal in sight has no real speed.

Midriver he stopped. He could hear nothing. "Kip?" he called.

No answer. Sound carried well over open water. It was not possible that Kip had not heard him. "Kip!" he shouted. No answer.

Con tread water.

There was no splashing sound. The river was eerily quiet, smooth as oil slicks.

"Kip!" he screamed.

Faintly he could hear water lapping the shore. Faintly, too, the repetitive drone of the *Duet*'s engines. If Kip was in the river, she, too, was treading water in silence. But Kip never played jokes. She did not have a mischievous bone in her over-achieving body. "Kip?" Con said. "Are you all right?"

* * *

Molly struggled to think up a logical fiction to explain why she was wearing somebody else's engagement ring. Blaze was already very edgy in this gathering of hostile strangers. If the girl he had just asked to squire him around town was in fact engaged to somebody who was not even here — who had not ever been mentioned — Blaze would vanish like rain in August.

Blaze didn't want a girlfriend. He just wanted fun. A temporary companion.

What is a friend? Molly thought. Do I have to have a yearlong calendar for a boy to qualify? Does he have to include school dances to count? Can you have a ten-day friendship? Would it be a waste of time? Was friendship ever a waste of time?

She was overwhelmed by a world of school that was gone, and a new world she seemed to have no access to. Thickly Molly Nelmes said, "Oh, this! Oh, Blaze. It's a good thing you noticed it. I had completely forgotten."

Blaze looked at the substantial, glittering diamond. It would be a hard thing for a girl to forget.

"It's my friend Emily's," Molly said. "She dropped it. I picked it up and put it on my hand for safekeeping."

Blaze did not have a girl's knowledge of rings to realize that dropping one's diamond ring was a rather unlikely event. He said, "Emily? Didn't I meet her?"

"Yes." Molly jumped up. "I'd better give it back now while I think of it. Come on."

What on earth do I say? she thought. What will Em and Matt say back to me? Does Matt even know?

Blaze took her hand. It was a sexless sort of thing, as if she were the teacher and he the child, and they were on their way to assembly. She yearned for the touch to be something more intense, to be far more than guidance. But what Blaze needed was a friend, not a girlfriend. Molly had been a girlfriend to more than she could count, but a friend — almost never.

How do I turn nice? Molly thought. Is it like turning a steak on the coals? Are you done on one side and raw on the other?

They found Emily and Matt alone in the dark beneath the dancers. The drums throbbed, their rhythm meeting the rhythm of the engines, so that the entire lower deck trembled. Molly's skull trembled with it, and her thoughts jounced.

She yanked the ring off her finger before Em and Matt noticed her. Blaze was obviously planning to enjoy himself. Probably figured he would be witness to a reunion between fiancée and ring, and everybody would cry with delight and hug each other forever.

Molly, who could crash any party and split any couple, was shocked to see Matt and

Emily. They were leaning on each other, and both their faces were wet, but with whose tears, she could not say. Sharing grief made them impenetrable. She could hardly step toward them. "Emily?" she said in a high voice completely unlike her usual bright, brittle tones.

Emily stared at her, expressionless. It was worse than a fierce expression. It was dead. Matt simply looked weary, as if he was worn down, and there was nothing left of him.

"I'm sorry I took so long," said Molly desperately. "You — you dropped your ring. I picked it up to give you and somehow it slipped my mind. Here it is. I know you must have been worried sick."

The ring was in the palm of Molly's hand. She held it out. The circle of gold gleamed, the diamond facing Matt.

Emily did not speak, did not reach for her ring, and did not look at any of them.

It was Matt who, tiredly, took the ring and told Molly how nice of her that was, how thoughtful, how very grateful he and Emily were to her. It sounded like memorized lines from an etiquette book. How to Thank the Person Who Brings Back Your Missing Jewelry.

Taking a breath so deep it could split lungs, Matt asked if Molly and Blaze would not like to join them.

"Oh, no, thanks, gee," said Blaze, horrified,

"that's nice of you, really, another time. Molly and I, well, we just made a special request of the band, and, um — "

"So we'll see you later," finished Molly, and she and Blaze stumbled away.

Tripping on each other and the shadows, they went back up, into the fresh river air, and the breeze. "What was that all about?" breathed Blaze.

"I think she broke up with him."

"I am so glad," said Blaze emphatically, "that I am going off to college. If I had to think of things like engagments and diamonds and marriage — " (he said this as if referring to death by dismemberment) " — I would collapse."

"So would Matt and Emily, I guess," said Molly. They walked up to the combo to request "Just the Way You Are," by Billy Joel.

She and Blaze danced, but only momentarily. "I'm not in the mood," said Blaze, so they sat.

"I'm glad I met you," he told her. "Westerly doesn't seem like such a dump anymore."

Molly laughed out loud. "Believe me, Blaze, it's still a dump. But I'm glad I'm the one who cheered it up for you."

He talked to her about New York, and college, and courses, but she didn't listen this time. She was remembering a plan that shot through her head back when she was following Kip, and figuring out that it had to be a surprise party for Anne. She had wanted enough time to buy Anne a good-bye present. Something really meaningful. She had had in mind baby clothes — just to remind the perfect couple of their not so perfect result.

". . . because there's so much action in a big city, and my parents liked the idea of a small men's college, but you know how it is. . . ."

I didn't do it, Molly thought. I didn't hurt Anne. I don't know if I can actually be your basic nice person, but at least I can ease off on being your basic mean person.

"What are you doing tomorrow, Blaze?" she interrupted him. "You've done the river now. Want to do the golf course at the country club?"

"Don't know how to golf."

"You live in a climate like Arizona and you don't golf? Sick. We have to fix that."

Blazed grinned. "Tomorrow then. Deal."

Deal, he said, not date.

Molly made a deal with herself. One date, one only, with Blaze, before he left. And he had to ask or it didn't count.

Chapter 20

Kip Elliott paused in midstream to orient herself. Her feet sank. She treaded water loosely.

Something hard and hooked grabbed her left ankle.

Kip didn't scream, only because she hated girls who screamed. She jerked her foot frantically and was pulled underwater. Then there was no scream because she had no air to scream with. She fought, hitting water, striking the river, trying to get free.

Every *Jaws*, *Jaws II*, and *Jaws III* rerun she had ever watched on television played before her. She would have no foot left, there would be blood roiling on the water, and incredible agonizing pain.

But nothing happened. Her foot remained prisoner and she ran out of air. Kip surfaced, nose barely above water, and sucked in air. Distantly she could hear Con calling her name. She had no time to worry about swimming contests.

I'm drowning, she thought.

Something is trying to drown me.

Kip tried to be rational. This was Westerly River. A flat, boring, current-free river with no menaces whatsoever. Her foot could not be moved. Kip took a deep breath, and ducked back underwater, prickling with terror, her air lasting far less time because fear took a lot of the oxygen for itself. She opened her eyes, but it was black as the sky above and she was blind. She surfaced again.

She was amazed how weakened she had become in only a few moments, her energy sapped by horror.

What is happening? Kip thought. She thrashed like an animal in a steel trap, trying to get free. Nothing happened.

She would have to get down to the level of her own ankle and see. Feel, actually.

Kip could not bear the thought of losing her fingers as well as her ankle. She found herself reconciled to going through life without her left foot, but a horror of her hands coming off made it impossible to dive down. She jerked herself backward, at every angle, but was pulled below the surface by the relentless grip on her foot.

A branch, she thought. It's a tree, washed downstream by the hurricane last fall. Low enough in the water that shallow-bottomed boats like the *Duet* never touch it, but my foot, pointing down as I tread water, lodged in a branch.

She pictured the tree, inanimate, unmoving, its own self stuck deeper down in mud. Mud, where it would lay Kip to rest with its ignorant, uncaring power. She imagined its bare branches, the fish swimming among them, the debris of old soda cans and tires caught like her ankle.

She saw her own death, her own body at the bottom.

Okay, all I have to do is lower myself, tug at the branches, and get my ankle loose, she said to herself. Piece of cake. Stay calm.

How easy it is to be the commander and order others to remain calm. How hard to be the one whose life is at stake and must obey the commander who says "Stay calm."

Kip dove under, trying to get at her own foot, but the water defeated her and washed her back, swirling her to the side. She might have thought the Westerly had no current, but all rivers flow, and she was very tired.

Surely just flexing the ankle, first left, then right, would have to free it from whatever notch it was caught in. Surely her own strength was enough to break the water-rotted twig that had her.

She flung herself in every direction, yanking and kicking and thrashing and wearing herself out. Above water, below water, hands reaching, fingers pulling.

Once more she heard Con's voice, and she

would have answered him this time if she could, but she could not find the strength.

She thought of tomorrow's local paper. She would be a headline. Next fall she would be a warning from the school principal to that year's students not to take silly risks. And that would be the sum total of Katharine Elliott's life.

Anne could not stop pacing around the tiny boat. With every step the *Duet* diminished, turning from a romantic party ship to a rowboat crammed with strangers.

And strangers they were.

She had never felt so isolated.

How totally your own life contained you, as if you were just so much Pepsi, locked in your own can. You sat on a shelf, and nobody could tell you from any other aluminum can.

There was Emily with Matt. There was Molly with the new boy. There was Beth Rose with her new boy. Con had literally swum out of her life.

Until Anne was pregnant, all those eons ago, she had felt like the most Belonging person in school. She belonged to the In group, she belonged to the cheerleading squad. She belonged to the Art Club and she belonged to the concert choir. Most of all, she belonged to Con, and therefore to that enviable group of girls who always had a date and were always wanted.

Pregnancy made her very different and if

you were different you could not belong. She frightened her friends by being what she was, and she terrified Con. Nobody could talk to her and nobody wanted to. She stood alone for a while and then it became unbearable; she accepted the offer of Beth's aunt to live with her until Afterward.

She acquired a whole new vocabulary to pretend that nothing was happening. When It was over, she would come home. And they would put It behind her, her mother liked to say.

But for Anne, It was always there. She carried It with her for nine months and when she signed the papers and gave away the baby she had held only moments, the knowledge of It was just as heavy.

She, actually. Not it. A little girl.

All the rest of her senior year Anne did not belong. She tried. Put It behind you, everybody said, and everybody else managed to. Anne did not. She was not another teenage girl; she was a mother herself. She was not Con's girlfriend, and he was not her date; he was the father of their child.

To belong — to belong!

She knew suddenly that the job had appealed to her because in crossing the world among strangers she did not have to pretend to belong, nor strive to belong. She would be isolated, in fact, and people would admire her for it. She and Miss Glynn would be a pair, bound by airline reservations and interview schedules. She would belong to a jet set in motion.

Even tonight, on this boat, at a party given for her, recipient of gifts, hugs, and kisses, Anne Stephens did not belong. They were all planning next year — dorms, roommates, courses, majors, vacations, letters. Even Emily or Molly, still in Westerly, still belonged. Westerly was always theirs, and they were always Westerly's.

The dark of the night and the dark of the river, the dark of the trees that came down the hills and closed in tight ranks along the banks of the river surrounded her.

And when I come back? Anne thought. Will I belong then? Will they take me back? Will they even be here in order to take anybody back? Will they all belong someplace else, or to somebody else?

What did it mean to belong? Or not to belong? And how much did she care?

She thought of the neat pile of passport, airplane tickets, and traveler's checks lying on her bureau, waiting for morning. In every journey, Anne thought, there is loss.

She wanted Con fiercely. Not to touch, and impossible to have. Just to be near, and remember when once she had belonged.

Anne walked back to the rail and said to Beth, "They've been gone a long time."

"Yes," Beth said, "we're starting to worry."

"Not to worry," ordered Jere, hoisting his

camera. "They'll appear the moment I take the lens cap off, I promise you."

Molly and Blaze joined them. Molly wanted to suggest that perhaps Kip and Con had decided to spend the night together on Swallow Island, but forced herself not to. Blaze chatted away, about how Molly was taking him to play golf on Sunday and would Jere and Beth Rose like to come along?

Beth gave Anne — not Molly — a long look.

I'm not worth looking at? Molly thought, the old rage percolating.

Jere said eagerly that that would be great, although he'd only been golfing once and would embarrass everybody. "You can't embarrass me," Blaze said. "I've never been golfing at all."

Molly hated how Beth and Anne were carrying on a personal conversation with their eyebrows, darting little looks of scorn Molly's way, announcing to each other that the idea of spending a Sunday with Molly was pitiful.

"Beth was telling me about how she's going to teach sixth grade," said Jere.

"We had that conversation, too," said Blaze.

Molly almost said how pathetic it was — everybody else discussing college, poor old worthless Beth stuck in elementary school. She curled her tongue on the roof of her mouth to stop herself.

"Why twelve year olds?" remarked Anne. "I hated sixth."

"You get the human body and blood and lungs," said Beth. "You get control of the multiplication tables at last. You're the big kids in the elementary school. You put on your first musical and study pyramids. I get all excited thinking about that whole year."

They laughed and Beth blushed. "Okay, so it's not much of a goal when other people want to be Hollywood directors or race car drivers," she admitted.

"Who wants to be a race car driver?" Blaze wanted to know.

"Rumor has it that Matt O'Connor is off to be a member of the pit team for Saylor Oil's racing cars."

Both Blaze and Jere were on their feet. "No! You're kidding! The lucky guy! I can't believe it. Which one is Matt O'Connor? I have to talk to him. Point him out!"

"He's the one we just talked to," Molly said.

Blaze stared at her. "The one you gave the diamond ring back to?"

Molly nodded.

Blaze and Jere abandoned Anne, Molly, and Beth Rose. They exploded on Emily and Matt like comets in the sky, shouting, "Really and truly? Pit crew? Races? Indy 500? Saylor Oil?"

Molly stood alone.

Anne and Beth drew together.

Molly felt like somebody from an entirely different race, or planet.

"What ring?" Anne said.

"You wouldn't believe it," Molly told her.

"I'd believe anything disgusting that you could get up to," Beth Rose snapped. "What on earth do you have to do with Emily's diamond ring?"

Molly turned away. Why tell them? They'd never believe it. She'd have to have lawyers, witnesses, sworn depositions, and even then Beth and Anne would refuse to believe that Molly ever did anything except to be mean.

"Did you try to steal Emily's ring?" Anne said.

Molly whirled on her. "Emily was so mad at Matt she threw it away, in your backyard, Anne Stephens, ten feet away from you, into your pretty little blue pool. You were too busy bragging about your Great Adventure. You never even saw Emily. She was crying all afternoon. She threw her ring away and I saw it fall and rescued it from the drain in the pool. And tonight when she and Matt were alone for a little while, I gave it back."

Anne and Beth Rose drew even closer together, and leaned in identical scornful positions against the brass rail. "A likely story."

Beth Rose took Anne by the shoulder and turned her like a mechanical doll to face the water instead of Molly. "Con and Kip will show up any second now," she said. "Let's call for them."

"Con!" shouted Anne.

"Kippie!" shouted Beth.

Molly shouted nothing. Her hatred came back deeper and fuller than ever before. Try to be nice and what happened? They pretended you didn't even exist.

Molly wanted to push them both overboard. Ruin their pretty hair, ruin their pretty little dresses, fill their mouths with polluted river water, and see them sink.

Chapter 21

They sat together. Matt did not ask Emily to put the ring on, and she did not ask to have it. Matt's hand lay limply in his lap.

He had thought, somehow, that if they could get the ring back — if they had it safe again; unthrown — he and Emily would be all right. What a superstitious thought, Matt realized. No circle of gold clutching a stone could change an argument. He wasn't quite so angry anymore; it had taken the financial part of his rage away.

But Emily was still hurt; he was still hurt; they still could not be at peace.

"I was just so mad at you!" cried Emily, stuffing her knuckles in her mouth to keep her voice down. "Everything fell apart inside me. You had better things to do. So big deal, we were going to have a wedding and a marriage. *You had a better offer.*" She took the ring from his curled hand and held it up to the light, like a fortune-teller with a glass ball. "So I threw it away from me, as hard and as far as I could."

"I didn't have a better offer," said Matt desperately. "I had a chance to try something first, Emily! A chance to see how good I am, whether I can be in a big league. You matter more than cars. You — " but he broke off. He had tried too often to tell her what he felt, and she could not, or would not, listen.

To his surprise, Emily slipped the ring back on her finger. She turned the stone inward, as if she did not want to look at it, and curled her fingers, keeping the ring in her own fist.

There was a pounding of feet. Boys leaped from gangways without using the steps, and heavy shoes hit the deck like bass drums. "Matt! Hey, Matt! Where are you?"

Matt and Em were startled, and got to their feet as if to ward off an attack. "I'm over here," called Matt, and instantly he was surrounded by Gary, Mike, Blaze, Jere, Donnie, Jason, Royce, and Mark.

"You really have a job like that?"

"Saylor Oil racing team?"

"Is that true?"

"When do you leave? Is it a permanent job? How did you get it? What are they paying you?"

The questions were thrown like hardballs, fast and excitedly. The boys made a wedge between Matt and Emily and she was pushed to the side. Matt thought, That'll be symbolic for Em. She'll say that's what the whole thing is — being pushed aside.

He ached, physically, to leap forward, like a chieftain at a bonfire, and shout in triumph what he had done, and what greater things were to come.

Emily had gotten stepped on. Her summer sandals were no match for the heavy shoes of a teenage boy. Wincing, she stood on one foot.

She thought, What is the matter with me? Look at him, on top of the world! And I'm going to say No? I'm going to push him down? He is the envy of everybody he knows, and he can't even answer them?

"Yes, it's true," said Emily. "Matt's leaving in less than ten days."

The boys whooped with excitement, clapping Matt on the back and demanding details. Matt's eyes went to Emily's.

"Looks like it's going to be one long engagement," she said to him softly.

"Yeah?" said Gary excitedly. "Why? How long is your job contract for, Matt?"

Emily had to laugh. Not one of the boys had thought of marriage when she used the word engagement. They assumed she meant Matt's job. Nothing else mattered to them.

It matters to me, she thought.

She turned the ring outward and went to find Molly.

"Yup. Pit crew," said Matt, squatting down, as if they were going to have an important huddle before the big game.

"We'll follow you across the country," Gary promised. "Name your race, we'll be there."

Emily left them. She found Molly stomping away from Anne and Beth Rose. Swallow Island to their right was a deeper black than the sky or river. "Molly," said Emily, giving her a hug, " I can't thank you enough."

Molly remained rigid, as though the hug belonged to somebody else and she was not going to get involved.

"I owe you so much," said Emily.

Molly pulled free.

Anne and Beth stared.

"Molly, don't go!" cried Emily. "I — well, I'm sorry Molly. All those times I should have given you the benefit of the doubt and didn't. Well — " Even to Emily this didn't sound very complimentary. Who wanted to be forgiven a nasty past? Nobody wants to hear they aren't so bad after all. People only want to be told they've been desirable all along.

Emily jumped sideways and blocked Molly's exit. "I'll be in Westerly, too, this year," she said. "And Matt'll be gone. He has a job with Saylor Oil's racing crew. He'll be all over the country. So let's — let's be friends."

Her foot came free.

Kip floated, panting, holding herself horizontal and very still, lest somehow she touch part of that horrible sunken tree again.

Rationally she knew exactly how deep the branches were. But her fear made it hard to kick or dip her arms. With baby splashes she tried to propel herself away.

"Kip!" shouted Con and she heard his powerful stroke coming her way. She found another particle of energy and got far enough from the tree that Con wouldn't get caught in it, too.

"Con," she croaked, "Con, help me!"

He was there. She clung to him as Kip had always refused to cling to anybody. "My foot. Caught on a tree branch underwater. I thought I would drown. I can't believe it happened to me. On my river!"

She was trembling with fatigue. "Stop swimming and hang onto me," said Con. "The *Duet* is just downstream, we'll be back on board in a heartbeat."

"I wasn't sure how many more heartbeats I was going to have," Kip panted. She let him support her, and her sodden hair rested on his cheek.

Kip's life, which had so annoyed him an hour earlier, took on a precious gleam. This brilliant, capable girl — probably the one in their entire class who really would accomplish great things — had nearly died at seventeen in a stupid accident. All that Kip could have done and been — gone. Foot caught underwater.

Anne's right, he thought, thinking not of Kip's hair and weight, but of Anne's. Do I really want to hold Anne's foot underwater? Yank her down to ordinary things when she can have the world?

The *Duet*'s engines rumbled smoothly. He could feel her vibrations in the water in which they hung.

The captain's huge shout rang through the night. "Kids!" he bellowed. "In the water! Diving off my boat? In the middle of the night? I'll never run a party of kids again. Stupid fools. Haul those two aboard! You idiots down there! You could have drowned!"

Chapter 22

America is a nation of moving vans. Parents are transferred, or want a larger house, or insist on a different school system. They want a new climate or to be farther from the city traffic, or closer to the city excitement.

But Anne, Emily, Beth Rose, Molly, and Kip had lived in Westerly all their lives. They had changed houses, but never towns. It was only in high school that they had gotten to know each other well.

And now, it seemed, they had hardly known each other at all.

Anne was only surprised that Molly had done nothing overtly cruel. It would have been Molly's style to get in touch with Ivory Glynn and tell her about Anne's past, explaining to the aging actress than Anne was not at all the sort of person Miss Glynn wanted around.

Beth felt it was bad enough that adorable Blaze had been taken up not by brilliant Kip but by rotten Molly. Blaze didn't even know she was rotten, he thought she was cute and funny. But worse than that, both Jere and Blaze thought Beth Rose was actually best friends with Molly! What a thought. But what could Beth do about it? Molly had set things up so it was difficult to let the boys know the truth unless Beth wanted to be pretty mean and bring up a lot of ugly stories about Molly.

Beth Rose and Anne turned their backs on Molly easily, because it was something they had done for years. Molly could crash all the parties she wanted, and on a boat where there was no point in raising a fuss, she could get away with it. But that did not, and never would, make Molly one of them.

Two friends shut out an unwanted third. It was a nice, powerful feeling — the solidarity of their backs, the power of exclusion. They pretended to search the glossy black water for signs of Kip and Con.

But it was Emily who materialized out of the night. Emily flinging herself on Molly, Emily begging for Molly's friendship, Emily crying Thank you, thank you! To Molly!

Emily hauled Molly over to Anne and Beth, to bring them into the celebration. Anne's yellow hair brushed against Beth's red mass of hair. When Emily reached them her own dark hair seemed as black as the night. Molly, hair shorter, skirt shorter, earrings longer, seemed part of another tribe.

"You see," cried Emily, her voice ringing with pleasure, "I did this stupid, childish, dumb, horrible, idiot thing."

Anne and Beth waited.

"I threw away my ring," said Emily.

Beth Rose stared at Molly. Molly had told the truth? Molly stared back, hostility and loathing written plain on her face.

"Matt's ring?" Anne repeated. She could no more imagine throwing away a diamond than throwing away a house.

Emily nodded. "Can you believe it? I'm the one who threw it away and *I* can't believe it. Thank heaven for Molly. You see, Matt is taking that job and he'll be gone for months at a time. I was so mad at him for abandoning me that —" she shuddered, remembering that furious act. "But Molly saved us," said Emily, smiling brilliantly at her.

Molly did not smile back.

Beth was aware that Jeremiah Dunstan had returned, complete with camera. He was getting every facial reaction, every line of dialogue. How obscene cameras are, thought Beth. Jere is catching us like prisoners. No matter how we change and grow, we will be trapped on that film, repeating this ugly encounter over and over.

I was the bad guy, Beth Rose thought. But

I'm always nice! I always forgive, I always help out, I always do the nice thing.

But it had never crossed her mind to believe Molly or to bother with Molly. Could Blaze after all, with the piercing sight that newcomers often have, be right? Could Molly be the girl worth knowing — and Beth the reject?

Molly was starting to leave. Beth could not let her go without saying something. But what? Beth took three difficult steps toward Molly, who backed off. Beth found herself playing to the camera — wanting to be sure that her moment of being nice was filmed, to offset her moment of being mean.

So why am I being nice? Beth asked herself. For Molly's sake? For my sake? For Jere's? For the audience that will see the film?

She had a curious surreal feeling she was actually behaving nicely for the *film itself*, as if she wanted the *camera* to think more highly of her.

Molly shrugged, making it clear that Beth's good behavior, or lack of it, was not one of Molly's interests in life.

The captain's bellow cut through the air. "Kids!?!" he screamed, as though he had just seen the most infuriating, disgusting spectacle of his life.

All kids on board immediately rushed to see what or whom could cause that bellow.

It was Kip and Con, treading water in the path of the *Duet*, waving frantically. The captain shouted with rage. Boys rushed to haul Kip and Con back on board. One of the crew brought blankets and another chewed Con out thoroughly for such stupidity, just the sort of thing they had expected from a conceited preppie jock with enough money to rent a whole boat for a whole night.

The party guests held their breath, half agreeing with the crew (who, after all, did not want to add two drowned teenagers to their accomplishments) and half dying to hear Con scream back.

But Con screamed nothing. Quietly he admitted, "We almost did drown. I'm sorry we scared you. We scared ourselves, too. It was pretty dumb."

Con Winter, being humble.

It silenced the entire boat.

From the upper deck came a high giggle. "Did you get that on film? We'll definitely want to show Con being humble at our reunion."

The party burst into laughter, and Con shook a fist lightly toward the teasing. The kids broke up into little groups once more, laughing, and speculating on what might have happened out on the water.

Beth touched Molly's shoulder. She hadn't finished her apology and Beth liked things neatly rounded off. "You see, I thought — " she began.

Molly interrupted her. "And you were right. I wasn't going to give the ring back. Does that satisfy you, Beth Rose Chapman? I *was* going to keep it. It isn't every day you acquire a free diamond. But — " Molly broke off. She spread her hands and looked at them, slim and long and lovely . . . and bare of rings.

So why did she do the right thing? Beth wondered. For Emily? For Matt? For herself? Or just because it was the right thing? Molly never noticed right from wrong before — why tonight?

The water churned behind the boat as they picked up speed again. Beth's thoughts churned in rhythm with it.

Jere said, "Beth, you look as if you're trying to decide the fate of nations."

Beth jumped. "No, just — " she collected herself, " — just the fate of our golf game. I want to go." She turned to Molly as if underlining this. "But you have that wedding appointment," Beth said to Jere.

"Wedding appointment?" said Emily. "You make it sound like a hair appointment."

"It's at four-thirty," said Jere. "How long can it take to play nine holes of golf?"

And Molly said to Beth, "Subtle, Beth."

"Well, I didn't want you to think — "

Molly broke into Beth's floundering speech. She had no patience with people who had to justify themselves and explain themselves and rattle on and on about something that was over and done with. "Nine?" said Molly. "You think we're going to stop with a piddly little nine holes? We're doing eighteen."

"Hey, great," said Blaze, getting all excited. "How much does it cost to rent clubs?"

"A fortune," Molly told him. "Bring tons of money. We want to have snacks and stuff at the clubhouse after."

"What if it rains?" said Jere.

"It won't."

"What do we wear?" said Beth.

"I have white jeans I like, and I'm sort of thinking of this turquoise-blue shirt. Women golfers wear little skirts but I like pants for any sports."

"Okay. I have white jeans, too." Beth thought, I always want everything to match. I want everybody to get along, and all jeans the same color, and all faces happy.

Matt had slipped back among them. Emily slipped her left hand into his right. Matt gripped it tightly, his thumb drawing back and forth over the rough facets of the stone in her ring. Emily leaned against him, and he pulled her in front of him, resting his chin in her hair.

"It'd be fun to go golfing with them. You don't mind do you? Shall we go, too?"

Emily nodded. She didn't expect Blaze and Jere to realize there was anything odd about Molly being the hostess, but she had thought Matt would at least show a little surprise. But boys never saw much. They never saw hostility among girls, or guessed at cliques that excluded, or spotted the layers of flirting and angling that each girl at the party could have described in detail.

She could feel Matt's satisfaction with life. The way he swayed her in front of him, the relaxed strength of his muscles, the easy voice with which he asked Molly for details. He had put their entire argument, all their pain, behind him. She, Emily, would turn the conversation and confrontation over in her mind a thousand times. Matt would simply accept that it was all okay now, and probably never think of it again.

Emily watched Molly. Molly's short hair was untouched by the night wind. She looked like a painted mannequin. Even her short skirt did not move, but stayed like plastic against Molly's legs. Molly's bright, brittle laugh rang like a doorbell.

So I am to be friends with Molly, Emily thought. What a strange turn of events.

She could tell Beth Rose was having an equally hard time with the concept, but Beth, being Beth, was trying very hard. Molly, being Molly, was laughing at her, and before long, the first thread of friendship would have snapped.

By September, Molly and Beth Rose and Emily would be the only ones left in Westerly. Perhaps the thread would not snap; perhaps they would need each other too much.

Emily was surprised to realize that she was just as relaxed as Matt. She thought, *I'm glad. Deep down, I think I wanted him to go! I didn't really want to start worrying about Tupperware and telephone bills, Ajax and mending. I think I wanted high school to go on forever — dating and playing games. Getting engaged was like playing a game.*

So Matt would go change tires at Daytona and at Lime Rock and Indianapolis.

And she — Emily — what would she do?

The world seemed full rather than lost. So full she could hardly think. First things first, thought Emily. Tomorrow, up at dawn. Golfing with Molly and Beth.

Chapter 23

Con finally located Anne. Not an easy task. She had removed herself entirely from everybody. "You're mad at me," he said lightly.

"You were always quick," Anne told him.

"I went swimming with Kip." Con was full of himself. He had understood a thousand important things out there in the river. He could hardly wait to share his new understanding, wonderful self with Anne. "Kip practically drowned," he told her. "She got her foot caught in a sunken tree branch. It really made me think."

"About what? Trees?"

"About us," Con said.

Anne sighed and moved fractionally away from him, surveying the shore, craning her neck to see if they were in sight of the dock yet. The bottom fell out of Con's self-confidence. Anne just wanted the party to end, so she could start her new life. Her better life. It's too late, thought Con, I left it until too late. "No," he said, "about the baby."

Anne sucked in her breath and stood very still.

"I'm sorry, Anne," he said. "You went it all alone, and I stayed as far off as I could. When Kip was drowning, though, I thought — I'm holding Anne's ankle under water, too. About Paris."

She smiled slightly. "Does this mean you're less upset that I'm going?"

"You were always quick," he said.

They were the same height, always at the same eye level. Con moved closer to her. He had so much to tell her, so many things that tonight, finally, he could admit. Could face.

But Anne's little smile remained untouched and unemotional. She said as soon as they docked could he please drive her straight home, because she needed a good night's sleep. "It was lovely of you to give me this party, and invite all my friends, Con," she said, as if thanking a stranger for picking up her dropped mitten. She looked around vaguely, but hardly including him in her glance. "Let's gather up the presents everybody gave me. And I've left my sweater someplace. Then we can go straight to the car."

"Anne, I want to talk. *Really* talk."

Her beautiful eyes stared into his. "But Con," said his girlfriend, and she was not being cruel, merely factual, "there's no time."

* * *

The boat docked with more of a jolt than anybody expected. They shrieked happily as they staggered to keep their balance. Ropes were flung and tied, the gangplank dragged out, and the party goers poured out onto dry land.

"Oooh, I'm still swaying!" cried one girl, as if they had all been on an ocean voyage for six months.

"It was a great party, wasn't it?" said a boy, fishing in his pockets for car keys.

"I wonder if we'll ever get together again for parties like this."

"Of course we will. Nothing will change."

They carried unfinished sodas, purses, towels, changes of clothing, bites of dessert snatched from the leftovers on the buffet. Anne had an armload, half of it dropping from her grip. Girls stooped to help her. A crowd headed for Con's car to dump the booty in his backseat.

"Hey! Don't leave yet!" cried Con. "More party to come!"

Anne turned. She looked at Con in complete exasperation. He knew the look well. I just told you I want to go straight home, and the first thing you do is announce More Party?

"See you next year, Anne!" shouted one group.

"Anybody need a ride? We have room for one more!"

"Don't forget to write."

In vain Con shouted for them all to come back. At last he turned. "Kippie," he said in his meekest, sweetest voice, "Kippie, do me one more favor. Please?"

"I can hardly wait till I'm in college and you can't hit me up for any more favors. I'll do this only because you held me up in the water. Although," she added, because Kip always liked the last word, "I did in fact save myself."

"Yes, you did," Con assured her. "You always will."

Kip raised her voice. She informed everybody they were to sit on the grassy bank facing the river. She wanted them bunched together and she wanted no nonsense about it, time was moving on.

There was instant obedience. People heading for their cars put their keys back in their purses and wheeled in a circle to go to the grassy bank.

"How do you do that?" Con said.

"Just bossy, I guess."

Con laughed. "Kip, I will miss you so much."

I will miss him, too, Kip thought. Conceited, annoying Con, I will miss him terribly. And Anne, and Emily, and everybody here! Kip's eyes grew misty.

She looked at the pairs around her — some that had lasted for years, some that began tonight.

Emily and Matt.

Anne and Con.

Beth Rose and Jere.

Molly and Blaze.

Only she, Kip was alone.

And I don't even care, she thought. Because it won't be for long. Boys in New York City have to be a hundred times more exciting than the ones I'm leaving behind in Westerly.

When the girls were together, they generally talked of the L word — a word conspicuously absent from most boys' vocabularies. Yet when Matt declared Love to Em, and gave her a diamond to prove it, Love seemed frightening. Kip and her friends weren't sure they wanted it after all.

Kip wanted Love on her own terms, according to her own description. She had scheduled it for New York.

Oh, Life! thought Kip Elliott, collapsing on the grass next to her friends. Here I come!

Beth Rose thought, I turned the corner and found not one, but two perfect boys. That won't happen again in this century. Of course one vanished in the blink of an eye and became Molly's. But the other is here beside me. And Jere lives in Westerly, goes to Westerly High. What if we date all year? I'll get to do my senior year over again!

More basketball play-offs. Another carnation day. A second senior prom!

She wondered how Jere would look in a tuxedo. If he knew what I'm planning for us, she thought, ducking her head so nobody could read her thoughts, he'd probably swim the Atlantic Ocean to escape. But I'm crafty. I'll sit here telling him what a great cameraman he is, and who knows?

"You look happy," Jere said.

People often informed Beth of this, slighty accusingly, as if she had no right to show any stray inexplicable happiness.

"What's so terrific?" asked Jere, true to form.

Beth smiled at him. "Life," she said. "I like it. I accept."

Molly Nelmes sat where, in her heart of hearts, she had yearned to be throughout the four years of high school. Among the In crowd. The Anne/Con crowd.

But high school was over and there was no longer a crowd to be part of or to get left out of.

I came too late, Molly thought.

Blaze said to her anxiously, "You'll be ready first thing in the morning? You won't be late?"

Molly laughed. Who cared about the past? She had Sunday to look forward to, and a week of Blaze's company. "I won't be late," she promised.

* * *

Anne Stephens' heart and mind and soul were singing the theme from *Annie*. *Tomorrow, tomorrow,* . . .

Con flopped on the grass, pulling her down into his lap. "We'll sit here," he commanded.

Oh, well, thought Anne, what's a few hours of sleep? The party can't last forever and even it if lasts till dawn, I can sleep on the plane.

Planes.

Anne pictured tomorrow. Collecting her passport, traveler's checks, tickets. Hand luggage and suitcases. Loading the car. Leaving plenty of time for traffic to the airport. Flight to New York. Disembark, take regularly scheduled bus-limousine service into Manhattan. Arrive at hotel. Meet Miss Glynn! Dress for dinner!

"What are you thinking of?" said Con in her ear.

"Tomorrow."

Con felt all the pain of being the one left behind, and Anne felt all the joy of the one going.

"Don't be mad at me," Con begged. "I'm kind of a nice guy, really, underneath it all."

The sky burst forth.

White stars exploded.

Galaxies shimmered and fell to earth.

Gold stardust quivered in a sooty sky.

"Fireworks?" Anne gasped. "Con! Is it some president's birthday I don't know about? How did you time it like this? Whose fireworks are they? Oh, Con, I *love* fireworks!"

One wonderful year Con had indulged her love of fireworks by driving her all over the state on the weekend of the Fourth, catching displays on Friday, Saturday, and Sunday night, early and late.

"They're your fireworks," said Con. "You're better than a president any day."

Anne made a face at him. "No, really."

"Yes, really. Look at the fireworks, Anne, not me. It's going to be a very quick show. I don't have as much money as the city of Westerly on the Fourth."

"How could you afford them?" Anne said suspiciously.

"I gave up my freshman year in college."

She laughed. "No, really."

"Yes, really."

A tympani roll of explosions shook the ground. An orange fireball exploded into falling stars that whistled as they flew through the sky.

"I thought there was a noise ordinance," Anne said.

"There is. I had to get a special permit."

"I beg your pardon," said Kip Elliott. "*I* had to get a special permit."

Anne was stunned. "You mean — Kip, tell me the truth. I can't trust Con. He really did this? For me?"

Kip nodded, smiling.

"Oh, Con!" Anne dissolved into tears. She ignored the spectacular sky and buried her face against his. "Con, it's perfect. To go out by fireworks!" She kissed him hard, and he returned it as intensely as he knew how.

The time for meaningful talks, for analysis and regrets, had gone by. Con had a terrible sense of what he had lost.

"Oh, Con," Anne said, "I'll miss you so much!"

There was no sentence he wanted to hear more. For if you cannot have your love, you want, at the very least, to be missed. To be a loss. To be thought of in other times, other places.

Ribbons of color streaked the sky and then vanished.

High school, and all their Saturday nights, had come and gone.

The party was over.

The air smelled of celebration.

Five girls went home to dream, to hope, to sleep.

The last summer night had ended.

...allow four to six weeks for delivery. Offer good in U.S.A. only. Sorry, mail ... orders are not available to residents of Canada. Prices subject to change.

point

Other books you will enjoy, about real kids like you!

☐ MZ43469-1	**Arly** Robert Newton Peck	$2.95
☐ MZ40515-2	**City Light** Harry Mazer	$2.75
☐ MZ44494-8	**Enter Three Witches** Kate Gilmore	$2.95
☐ MZ40943-3	**Fallen Angels** Walter Dean Myers	$3.50
☐ MZ40847-X	**First a Dream** Maureen Daly	$3.25
☐ MZ43020-3	**Handsome as Anything** Merrill Joan Gerber	$2.95
☐ MZ43999-5	**Just a Summer Romance** Ann M. Martin	$2.75
☐ MZ44629-0	**Last Dance** Caroline B. Cooney	$2.95
☐ MZ44628-2	**Life Without Friends** Ellen Emerson White	$2.95
☐ MZ42769-5	**Losing Joe's Place** Gordon Korman	$2.95
☐ MZ43664-3	**A Pack of Lies** Geraldine McCaughrean	$2.95
☐ MZ43419-5	**Pocket Change** Kathryn Jensen	$2.95
☐ MZ43821-2	**A Royal Pain** Ellen Conford	$2.95
☐ MZ44429-8	**A Semester in the Life of a Garbage Bag** Gordon Korman	$2.95
☐ MZ43867-0	**Son of Interflux** Gordon Korman	$2.95
☐ MZ43971-5	**The Stepfather Game** Norah McClintock	$2.95
☐ MZ41513-1	**The Tricksters** Margaret Mahy	$2.95
☐ MZ43638-4	**Up Country** Alden R. Carter	$2.95

Watch for new titles coming soon!
Available wherever you buy books, or use this order form.

point ® **THRILLERS**

☐ MC44330-5	**The Accident** Diane Hoh	$2.95
☐ MC43115-3	**April Fools** Richie Tankersley Cusick	$2.95
☐ MC44236-8	**The Baby-sitter** R.L. Stine	$3.25
☐ MC44332-1	**The Baby-sitter II** R.L. Stine	$3.25
☐ MC43278-8	**Beach Party** R.L. Stine	$2.95
☐ MC43125-0	**Blind Date** R.L. Stine	$3.25
☐ MC43279-6	**The Boyfriend** R.L. Stine	$3.25
☐ MC44316-X	**The Cheerleader** Caroline B. Cooney	$2.95
☐ MC45401-3	**The Fever** Diane Hoh	$3.25
☐ MC43291-5	**Final Exam** A. Bates	$2.95
☐ MC41641-3	**The Fire** Caroline B. Cooney	$2.95
☐ MC43806-9	**The Fog** Caroline B. Cooney	$2.95
☐ MC43050-5	**Funhouse** Diane Hoh	$2.95
☐ MC44333-X	**The Girlfriend** R.L. Stine	$3.25
☐ MC45385-8	**Hit and Run** R.L. Stine	$3.25
☐ MC44904-4	**The Invitation** Diane Hoh	$2.95
☐ MC43203-6	**The Lifeguard** Richie Tankersley Cusick	$2.95
☐ MC45246-0	**Mirror, Mirror** D.E. Athkins	$3.25
☐ MC44582-0	**Mother's Helper** A. Bates	$2.95
☐ MC44768-8	**My Secret Admirer** Carol Ellis	$2.95
☐ MC44238-4	**Party Line** A. Bates	$2.95
☐ MC44237-6	**Prom Dress** Lael Littke	$2.95
☐ MC44884-6	**The Return of the Vampire** Caroline B. Cooney	$2.95
☐ MC44941-9	**Sister Dearest** D.E. Athkins	$2.95
☐ MC43014-9	**Slumber Party** Christopher Pike	$3.25
☐ MC41640-5	**The Snow** Caroline B. Cooney	$3.25
☐ MC43280-X	**The Snowman** R.L. Stine	$3.25
☐ MC43114-5	**Teacher's Pet** Richie Tankersley Cusick	$2.95
☐ MC43742-9	**Thirteen** Edited by T. Pines	$3.50
☐ MC44235-X	**Trick or Treat** Richie Tankersley Cusick	$2.95
☐ MC43139-0	**Twisted** R.L. Stine	$3.25
☐ MC45063-8	**The Waitress** Sinclair Smith	$2.95
☐ MC44256-2	**Weekend** Christopher Pike	$2.95
☐ MC44916-8	**The Window** Carol Ellis	$2.95

Available wherever you buy books, or use this order form.